DAYS OF GOLD

Ardyce Czuchna-Curl

8/29/05

Life is an Adventure !
Enjoy this one with Marianne
& Thomas .

Ardyce Czuchna-Curl

Oak Woods Media

Oak Woods Media
PO Box 19127
Kalamazoo MI 49019
(616) 375-5621

Illustrations by Robert Lawson

Printed in the United States of America
with soy-based ink on recycled paper

First edition

Although this is a work of fiction, the times and places
are historically authentic.

Library of Congress Cataloging-in-Publication Data
Czuchna-Curl,Ardyce, 1934-
  Days of Gold / Ardyce Czuchna-Curl
    p. cm.
  Summary: At the beginning of the Klondike gold rush in
1897, twelve-year-old Marianne and fourteen-year-old Thomas
set out on a perilous journey from Seattle to the gold fields in
search of their father.
  ISBN 0-88196-012-8
  1. Klondike River Valley (Yukon)–Gold discoveries–Juvenile
fiction. [1. Klondike River Valley (Yukon)–Gold discoveries–
Fiction. 2. Brothers and sisters–Fiction. 3.Voyages and travels–
Fiction. 4. Canada–History–1867-1914 Fiction.] I.Title.

PZ7.C99917 Day 2002
[Fic]–dc21   2002016954

Acknowledgements

This story grew out of my work at Klondike Gold Rush National Historical Park in Skagway, Alaska in 1996 and 1997. Hiking much of the Chilkoot Trail led me to read diaries and accounts of the lives of people who had traveled the same route a hundred years before.

Thanks to colleagues in my Kalamazoo and Battle Creek writers' groups, to members of the Society for Children's Book Writers and Illustrators and to Laura Armstrong for listening, critiquing, and encouraging me. Thanks to children of Portage, MI, McKinleyville, CA, and Eagle and Skagway, AK for their enthusiastic reception of early drafts. Thanks also to Cathy Cook and Karl Gurcke of the National Park Service and to Judy Munns of the Skagway Museum for research help.

But the most gratitude must go to my husband, David, who has supported me and encouraged me to complete this book and let it fly.

For Sarah

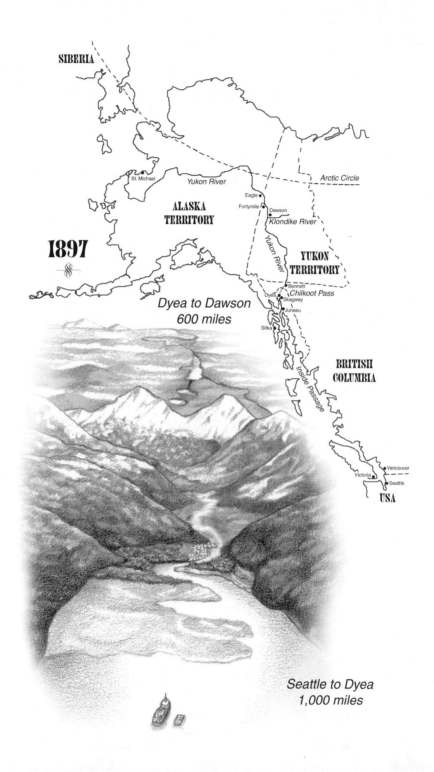

SIBERIA

St. Michael

Yukon River

ALASKA
TERRITORY

1897

Arctic Circle

Eagle

Fortymile

Dawson

Klondike River

Yukon River

YUKON
TERRITORY

Bennett

Dyea

Chilkoot Pass

Skagway

Juneau

Sitka

Dyea to Dawson
600 miles

Inside Passage

BRITISH
COLUMBIA

Vancouver

Victoria

Seattle

USA

Seattle to Dyea
1,000 miles

Chapter 1
SEATTLE
September 1, 1897

T he whistle blasted. The ship was ready to sail, but Thomas had disappeared. Struggling with Grandmother's big leather valise, Marianne wished she hadn't brought her favorite doll, Sophia.

"Twelve-year-olds are too big for dolls," her brother had said. But she couldn't leave Sophia behind. Grandmother had given her the doll just before she died.

Marianne searched the crowd for her brother. He'd said he'd meet her by the gangplank as soon as he'd loaded their gear.

"Since I have a job with the crew, I can put our stuff on the ship for free," Thomas had told her. "And I had to buy only one ticket—one for you."

Passengers already aboard were waving to friends and family on shore. Amidst all of these people, Marianne's head pounded. I can't get on the ship without Thomas, she thought, brushing back tears.

The ship's whistle blew again. I have to get on, or I'll be left behind, she reasoned. Pushing through the crowd, Marianne hurried up the gangplank. Men and women jostled for space for themselves and the boxes and baskets they carried. An elbow jabbed

Marianne in her ribs. She struggled to breathe. Hoards of people, most of them taller than she, surrounded her. The mingled smells of cigar smoke, perspiration and camphor made her dizzy.

Marianne stared at men in dark woolen coats and suits and soft felt fedoras, stiff rounded derbies or billed caps. None look like they were dressed to mine for gold, she thought. If Thomas wasn't on board how would she be able to manage among all those strangers?

She looked for a space on deck. Finally, spotting an opening, she wedged herself between two families. A young woman, nursing a child, was crooning a lullaby. A clean-shaven man on his knees was spreading a blanket over them.

"Don't cry now, Robby," the man said as he handed a cracker to the toddler tugging on his shirtsleeve.

On the other side of Marianne a woman passed out pieces of cold potatoes to three children. "Don't worry, my pets," she said, wiping a tear from the face of a little girl. "We'll soon be with Daddy. He's making a home for us."

Home, thought Marianne. This ship would be her home for a week. Leaving home and friends seemed so final.

"With Grandma gone, there's nothing to keep us in Seattle," Thomas had said. "We have to find Papa."

Her stomach churned. She felt so alone. Perhaps she would never return.

Yes, she thought. We do have to find Papa, but right now there's just *me*.

Setting her jaw, she decided she would not go north without Thomas. He was only fourteen, but Marianne looked to him as a grownup. She would

stay in Seattle where at least things were familiar.
She turned and tried to push her way back toward
the gangplank. But the ship was moving. Looking
back at the city's skyline, Marianne watched the tall,
brick buildings become smaller as the ship, belching
smoke, moved out of the Seattle harbor. There was
no turning back now.

Without Thomas I'll be alone in a strange place
without food, friends or a roof over my head. Maybe
I could find a job, but I'll never find a friend like
Sarah. And if a letter comes from Papa, it may never
catch up with me.

I'll have to wait 'til more folks are settled before
I look for Thomas, she thought. The knot in her
stomach tightened.

Pushing herself back into the space she had
earlier claimed for herself and Thomas, Marianne sat
down on the deck. It seemed colder than it had
before. She hoped Thomas would have an extra
blanket.

"Don't take anything you don't absolutely need,
he had said." Seeing the doll, he had complained,
"Leave her behind," but Marianne had held her
ground. She also was glad she had thought to bring
Grandma's woolen cape. It was going to be cold on
the ship.

Waves splashed against the vessel, a child whim-
pered, and a woman hurried to the side of the boat
to throw up. Marianne, feeling confined and stifled,
wiped tears from her eyes, held Sophia close, and
tried to relax.

She smoothed her own twill skirt and wrinkled
white poplin shirtwaist. The blouse would be black
with soot and dirt before they got to Dyea. She
checked the buttons on her leather boots. She was

glad when she last shopped for shoes her grandmother had insisted she buy sensible ones. The
patent leather pumps she had admired would never
do for this trip.

Marianne wondered what the Klondike was
really like. She had heard it was an exciting new
place—with lots of people pushing to find gold.
Even the mayor of Seattle had left his job to head for
the gold fields. But Marianne didn't know where her
father was, and now she was afraid she'd lost Thomas too.

Chapter 2
THE SHIP

S he looked up at the sound of her name.
"Marianne!" Thomas waved wildly from the
upper deck.

"Up here, Marianne!" he shouted.

Setting the doll aside, Marianne stood up and
waved back. "I'm coming, Thomas."

Tiptoeing around the sleeping children and
ignoring the grumbling voices of some of the
grownups, she made her way toward her brother.

Reaching Thomas, she hugged him. "Thank
goodness I found you. Are you all right? Did you get
all of our things aboard?"

"I'm fine. Yes, I got all our stuff on the ship.
They let me stow our extra food below, but it took a
long time to haul it there. Sorry I couldn't get back
to meet you. I had to count on finding you after the
ship cast off."

"And what if I hadn't been here?"

"You know I would have found you."

"I guess," she said as she tossed her brown hair
behind her. Her stomach was still doing flip-flops,
but at least she and Thomas were together.

"It's scary, isn't it?" she said looking out across
the water.

Thomas shrugged.

He's scared too, Marianne thought, but he's not letting on. "I wish I knew more about the Klondike," she said, shifting attention away from their fears.

Thomas wrinkled his forehead. "The Klondike is a lot of men and women stampeding for gold, I guess. But come on. Let's get settled. Help me carry what we'll need while we're on the ship." He guided Marianne to a large canvas bag and a wooden box. "Let's take these to the spot you've staked out."

They made their way through rows of passengers huddled together trying to stay warm and holding a claim to their space. Amazingly, there was still room where Marianne had left her belongings. And Sophia. Marianne's heart lurched, but she relaxed when she saw the doll's leg sticking out of Grandma's leather valise. She checked the contents—a change of underwear and stockings, notepaper, pencil, comb with missing teeth, washcloth, towel, dried fruit, crackers and cheese. Everything seemed to be there.

Thomas motioned for Marianne to sit. "Stretch out your legs," he said, "or we'll lose our space and have no room to breathe."

"It does feel good to stretch," she said.

As darkness moved over them, they gazed up at the stars.

"Hey, there's the Big Dipper." Thomas pointed at the constellation. "Did you know the two stars farthest away from the handle point toward Polaris, the North Star?"

"How do you know that?" Marianne asked.

"Papa taught me. He said that before the compass was invented, the North Star was the best guide for travelers. We'll be heading north all the way to the gold fields."

"I hope we don't have to use the North Star to guide us to Papa."

"Don't worry, Marianne, I'll take care of you," her brother promised.

Yes, she thought, —if I can keep track of you.

Settling down to watch the night sky, Thomas continued with explanations. "There's Orion the hunter," he said. "Notice the three stars in a row that form his belt. And, over there, that group of stars shaped like the letter *W* is Cassiopeia."

Marianne repeated the strange names to herself, wishing she had paid more attention when Papa had pointed out stars. She'd been too busy playing with Sophia.

Finally, pulling out the gold watch that had been their grandfather's, Thomas said, "It's nearly 11 o'clock. I have to go to work, but I'll be back before you wake up." He left his duffel bag beside Marianne to reserve his sleeping space.

I hate being alone all night, Marianne thought; but to Thomas she said, "Be careful. I don't want you to fall overboard."

"You worry too much, Marianne," her brother chided. "And you're hardly alone." He turned to make his way through the crowd.

I do worry, Marianne concluded, as she looked about her. People were wedged together like cords of wood. She huddled against the side of the ship, drew Grandma's woolen cape over herself and her doll, and tried to sleep. The water lapped against the side of the ship. The stars twinkled. Gradually Marianne's eyelids closed.

Next morning the stench of vomit and perspiration permeated the air.

"I think I am going to throw up," Marianne said to Thomas who had crept back to his spot near her in the early hours of the morning. "And I'm freezing. I'm going below where it's warmer."

"Better stay up on deck in the fresh air," Thomas cautioned. "The sailors say the ones who get seasick are those who go below. Some may be sick the whole trip. Besides, dozens of cattle, about a hundred horses and a flock of sheep are down there. The animals don't even have room to lie down."

To keep her mind off the unpleasantness, Marianne thought of her friend Sarah and the good times they'd had trying on hats in Sarah's mother's millinery shop and munching crisp crackers from the barrel in Grandma's store. They'd played hopscotch, jumped rope on the sidewalk, and held tea parties for their dolls in the back room of the hat shop.

The sound of a baby crying brought Marianne back to the present. As they entered what the sailors referred to as the Inside Passage, the water became calm. Seagulls hovered near the ship.

"Look at that eagle," Thomas pointed out. Marianne craned her neck and strained her eyes until she spotted a white head at the top of a tree. Deep green forests seemed to go on forever. Marianne saw no sign of humans along the rocky shoreline.

"There's a humpback!" someone shouted. "Starboard side." Watching passengers rush to the right side to get a view of the huge sea creature, Marianne was afraid the ship would tip over. Luckily, she was near the railing and could easily watch the show.

The whale glided through the glassy water, its

gray skin gleaming in the sunlight. As it arched its back and dipped in and out of the water, Marianne began to understand why these gigantic mammals were called humpbacks.

The third morning of the voyage Thomas was breathing hard when he returned from his shift.

"Marianne, come by the stairway where we can talk privately," he whispered.

"Look what I've found," he said, when they were away from the crowd.

Marianne stared as Thomas pulled a fat roll of bills from a small leather bag.

"Hundreds of dollars!" she gasped. "Where did you find all that money?"

"In the stairway."

Examining the bag, her heart pounding, Marianne saw that it was hand stitched on the edges; a buffalo head had been branded onto the front.

"We have to find the owner."

"There's no name in the pouch," Thomas said. "With this money we could buy the supplies we'll need. We could head up the trail right away. I wouldn't have to get a job and earn money first."

"Well, we *are* going to need boots and jackets and rain gear," Marianne agreed. "With the extra money we could get to Dawson City sooner to look for Papa. Still, it's not right."

"Don't be silly, Marianne. This is a windfall."

"Thomas, we can't keep the money. We have to find out whose it is."

"If we announced we had found a money pouch, guess how many folks would claim it?" Thomas countered. "There are two hundred people on this ship."

"If only the owner had put his name in it,"
Marianne said.

Chapter 3
THE MONEY
September 4, 1897

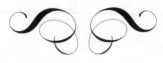

Marianne's muscles ached from sitting in the same cramped position for hours. She thought of her warm bed back in Seattle as she prepared for her morning walk and she worried about the moneybag Thomas had hidden amongst his things. But while Thomas was here on deck to watch her valise and his duffel bag and to protect their space, this was a good time for her to look around.

It was difficult to work her way among all of the people, but she did her best to circle the ship, even though she had to step over sleeping passengers.

On her trek around the ship the day before, she had noticed a bearded man, wearing a black-and-red-plaid wool shirt, also attempting a stroll on the deck. He had smiled at her. Somewhat older than her father, but very handsome, she had thought. He had looked more confident and less frenzied than many of the other passengers.

Suddenly, she was hungry. She headed down to the food line on the deck below. This morning she noticed the bearded man again, but now he was searching through his pockets, shaking his head and muttering to himself: "Where is it? I can't believe I dropped it. How could I have been so careless?"

Marianne froze. Did the money belong to him? If it did, they must return it. But she had to be sure. She decided to follow him. He headed for the galley, poured himself a mug of coffee and sat sipping and shaking his head.

By now most of the passengers had eaten, so the food line was mercifully short. Marianne dropped a coin in the canister set out for that purpose, held out her tray, and the server flapped three pancakes on it. Another helper sprinkled sugar and cinnamon on top of the cakes, while a third pushed a slice of bacon onto the tray. Marianne helped herself to a cup of hot cocoa and headed for a spot at the long table where she could keep an eye on the man. After awhile, he drained his cup, rose and walked out of the galley.

Leaving a pancake on her plate, Marianne headed in the direction the man in the plaid shirt had gone. She found him standing in front of the purser's counter. The purser was shaking his head. Moving closer, Marianne could hear part of the conversation.

"No? No, I don't suppose anyone did turn it in. I was a fool to carry all of my cash in that bag. If it shows up, hang onto it. I'll check back later. Thanks."

The man in the plaid shirt headed toward the upper deck. Marianne's throat was dry and her stomach queasy. She wanted to run after the man and say, "We found your money;" but first, she'd have to talk to Thomas.

When she told Thomas what she'd heard, he sighed. "I suppose you want to give the bag to him."

"Of course," she said. "What if the money had been ours?"

Thomas thought for a moment. Finally, he said, "Dang it, I guess you're right. We'll have to give it up. But let's be sure the money belongs to him."

Marianne had little doubt herself, but if Thomas wanted more time....

That night after Thomas went to work, Marianne tossed and turned as the boat rocked to and fro. Passengers gagged and vomited. *The money belongs to him. Give it back. Give it back. It's not yours. Sure you could use it, but it's not yours. Give it back. We will give it back. Just give us time.* She awoke in a cold sweat, dressed and hurried to take her walk while most of the passengers were still sleeping. Also taking his walk as usual was the man with the plaid shirt. This time he spoke to her.

"Good morning, Miss. How are you this beautiful morning?"

Beautiful morning? She wondered how he could call this a beautiful morning when he had lost hundreds of dollars. Perhaps he wasn't the one who had dropped the bag after all.

"I'm well, thank you," she said, not meeting his eyes. "I'm glad I'm not sick like many of these passengers."

"Yes, I'm kept busy tending them. I just get to sleep and someone wakes me."

"Are you a doctor?"

"Yes, and also a sailor and a cook—sort of a jack-of-all-trades. But not a very good bill collector, though."

Marianne wondered what he meant by that, but decided she shouldn't ask any more questions. She continued her walk. If he knew they had found his money, she and Thomas might be arrested. Taken to prison. But we *found* the money. We didn't steal it.

The next morning, Marianne stood on the deck watching for wildlife. She was absorbing the view of lush green forests when a conversation attracted her attention. She pretended to concentrate on the seagulls flying overhead.

"Yes, I'd planned to go on to stake a claim," the bearded man said. "But now I'm not sure I can. I've lost my grubstake. If I could get to Bennett, I could build boats and earn enough for a new grubstake. Lots of folks don't know how to build boats. I helped build several while growing up on my father's schooner off the coast of Massachusetts."

Marianne wanted to say, "We found your money bag." But Thomas said they must be absolutely sure who it belonged to. She turned and hurried back to Thomas.

Her brother was sleeping, exhausted from his night job. He'd started out peeling potatoes and setting up utensils for the morning meals, but lately the chief steward had decided Thomas was strong enough to do more strenuous tasks. Thomas needed his rest. Marianne would talk to him later.

After pushing her way between the two families with small children, she drew the cape around herself and settled down for a nap. It wasn't bedtime, but there was little to do but look at the scenery or sleep. It was a long time before she slept. *...You've stolen my money. Where did you put the moneybag? Why didn't you turn it in to the purser? You know it's not your money. Bring it back.*

Chapter 4
DOC
September 7, 1897

T homas was shaking her.

"Wake up, Marianne." This is the day we get to Dyea."

Marianne, who had been counting the days, jumped up and gathered her belongings.

"I have to find someone to hire to help us load our gear onto one of those barges, so we're ready to go in to shore at high tide," Thomas was saying. "This ship can't get into port because the water's so shallow."

"We have to pay more money? I thought my ticket would take care of everything."

"Nope. Remember I told you we have to haul our own gear or pay someone to do it? If you can carry your valise and my duffel bag, I'll see that the other things get loaded onto one of those barges."

"Thomas, I had an awful nightmare. I dreamed someone knew we had the money."

"Hush," whispered Thomas. "Don't even think about it."

But she couldn't *not* think about it.

Now remembering the conversation she had heard earlier, she had an idea. "Thomas, you said that after we leave Dyea and get over the mountains, it's

more than 500 miles to Dawson City, and we're
going to need a boat to get there."

"Yeah, you're right."

"Well, I know someone who could build one."
She paused.

"I'm listening."

"The man who lost the money. Maybe he'll
help us build a boat when we get to Bennett. He
might even help us unload our stuff here at Dyea."

"Are you sure he can build boats?"

"He said he had helped build several."

"Where is he?"

"I'll be right back," Marianne said before Thomas
could change his mind. She headed for where she
usually walked. There he was, but at the rail staring
at the coastline instead of walking.

Near the shore a circling eagle perched high in
a spruce tree. Harbor seals sunned themselves on
the rocks. Someone paddled close by in a log canoe.
One of the crewmen said the ship was entering the
Taiya Inlet.

Marianne braced herself.

"Sir," she began in a soft voice. Then she cleared
her throat and spoke a bit louder. "Sir."

After what seemed a long time, the man turned.
"Yes? What is it?" He smiled pleasantly.

"Did you lose a bag?"

He cocked his head and looked at her curiously.
"Why do you ask?"

"Because we found one. Can you describe your
moneybag, Mr. ... er?"

"Charles Elliott. They call me Doc." He put out
his hand and they shook.

"I'm Marianne Carson."

He continued, "In answer to your question, the

bag is a brown leather one bound with tan stitches with a buffalo head branded on the front. It contains a big roll of bills, more than a thousand dollars."

"Then the one my brother found must be yours," Marianne said. "Come and meet Thomas."

The man clapped his hands. "You found it? Such good news! I may get to the gold fields after all."

He followed her. As always, they had to push through a crowd. Thomas was studying some sketches of boats he had scrawled on an old tablet. He rose when he saw Marianne and the man.

"This is my brother Thomas," Marianne said. "This is Doc Elliott."

The two shook hands.

"I'm glad to meet you, Thomas. I understand you found my bag."

Thomas looked at Marianne, shrugged and then reached into his gear, pulled out the bag and handed it to Doc.

"I'm delighted to get this back!" Doc looked from Marianne to Thomas. Then he cocked his head. "The money's been missing several days. What made you decide to return it now?"

"Marianne thought it was yours right away," Thomas said. "But I wanted to be sure, so she did some investigating."

"I appreciate your caution. Now until I can reward you properly, how about I help you two get your goods to shore?"

Thomas hesitated.

"Oh, that would be wonderful," Marianne said.

"We could use some help, sir," Thomas added.

Marianne realized she'd been holding her breath. Now she exhaled slowly. Things were going to work out—maybe.

Chapter 5

DYEA

G oing ashore wasn't easy. The captain
dropped anchor in the bay, far from shore
next to a big flat boat. Men and women
struggled to unload their goods onto the barge.
Lumber, bales of hay, drums of kerosene and kegs of
whiskey were thrown overboard on the incoming
tide. Marianne shivered as sheep, dogs and cattle
were dumped into the icy water and forced to swim,
bleating, barking and mooing as they scrambled for
footing. Frightened horses were swung over the side
of the ship in slings.

After six hours, the tide had gone out again and
dropped thirty feet, grounding the barge. The
steamer had sailed away, and the inlet was a sea of
mud. The animals' owners chased their stock toward
dry land.

Marianne sat on one of their packing crates.
Her clothes were spattered with mud. Her feet were
wet. She was cold, tired and thirsty and she wondered where she would sleep that night.

Why she had left Seattle for this, she could not
imagine. Yes, Thomas and she had been alone there,
but at least they had a roof over their heads. Many
folks were out of work because the country was in

what Grandma had called a depression, but they could have found work, maybe. "There's always work for those willing to do it," Grandma had said.

Marianne watched as Doc hailed a wagon driver and bargained with him to move their goods before the next tide. Fortunately, the wagon was large enough to carry all of their belongings ashore through the mud flats. Thomas helped Doc load their stuff onto the wagon and then beckoned Marianne to come along.

"I can't imagine how we'd have managed if Doc hadn't helped us," Marianne said as they followed the wagon carrying their bags of flour and oatmeal and other supplies.

"We'd have done it, but this sure was easier," Thomas admitted.

So this was Dyea! Marianne stared at food and blankets, sleds and stoves, portable pianos and casks labeled "medicine" piled up on the ground. Sacks and bags were stacked as far as she could see.

Tents, many of them saloons, lined the shore. Farther away from the beach, clapboard hotels, log cabin restaurants and other unpainted buildings stood along the muddy trail leading toward the mountains. Dozens of men hurried back and forth, checking and rechecking their goods. Animal cries and human curses filled the air. Bags, crates and barrels were stacked everywhere.

"Where did all of these folks come from?" Marianne asked as she, Thomas and Doc tromped through the mud amidst a sea of tents.

"From all over the country," Doc said. "Many are from Seattle, of course, like you and Thomas; but some are from as far as the east coast—others are from foreign countries.

"Let's set up camp here," Doc said when they finally came to an open space. Immediately Thomas pulled out canvas, rope and wooden pegs; and they proceeded to put up the tent. Marianne removed her boots and stuffed paper inside of them to help them dry quickly as her grandmother had taught her.

"We never could have made it without you," Marianne said to Doc. "Thank you so much."

Thomas gave her a *We would have managed somehow* look, as he pulled out his rifle and laid it on top of their large knapsack.

"Careful with that gun, son," Doc exclaimed.

"Yes, sir," Thomas said. "My pa taught me how to use it." He caressed the gun.

"One can't be too careful," Doc said. "Now you pound in the tent pegs while I stretch out this canvas."

Marianne opened a tin box containing food-stuffs. She supposed she'd be the cook and wondered what she should fix for dinner. While she looked through the box of provisions, Thomas and Doc finished setting up her and Thomas's tent. Then Thomas helped Doc set up his tent next to theirs.

That evening as Marianne tossed bacon pieces into the pot where the white beans simmered, she was glad she had often helped her grandmother with the cooking. "Learn to cook, Marianne," Grandma had said. "You never know when you may have to feed yourself."

Now, having built a fire by herself in the make-shift iron stove Thomas had concocted, Marianne gradually became comfortable in her new role.

Bacon would give the soup flavor. Then, re-membering the onions in their pack, she quickly peeled and cut up one and tossed the slices into the kettle. This soup might not be as good as Grandma's, but it would have to do.

"Mm, that sure smells good," Doc said as he came near the stove. He was wearing his usual plaid shirt, but he had trimmed his graying beard and combed his hair. He smiled at Marianne.

"Wouldn't sourdough bread taste good with that soup?" he asked.

"I don't know how to make bread," Marianne said.

"Well, you soon will. Look, I brought you a present." Doc opened a sack of flour. Marianne peered into the bag. Nestled in the flour was a glob of grayish liquid, bubbling quietly.

"Ugh," Marianne said. Then remembering her manners, she said, "I mean, thank you. What is it?"

The doctor laughed. "Sourdough. I carry the starter in the flour sack so it won't get spilled or dry out. It also keeps warm in there. Some fellows carry theirs inside their shirt, under their armpits."

"I think I'm going to throw up."

Doc chuckled; then seeing the dismay on Marianne's face was real, he sobered.

"Here, I'll show you how to use it," he said, removing his jacket. "First, set aside a cupful of the starter and guard it with your life. It could *save* your life someday. Let me have that crock. And a wooden spoon. Never use metal because sourdough takes on a metallic taste. We'll put the extra starter in that crock and save it for the next time you make bread, rolls or pancakes. Every few days you'll need to add about a half-cup of flour and a half-cup of water and a dash of sugar to the starter to keep it active.

"Now, would you hand me some sugar?" Doc stirred the mixture thoroughly; then he greased another crockery bowl and placed the sourdough in it and set it on the crate Marianne provided.

"Let it rise until it's doubled in bulk," Doc said. "Then knead it down. Let it rise to double bulk again. Then form it into a loaf, and bake it about forty-five minutes in a hot oven.

"I have to go and check on a patient. I think I'm the only doctor in Dyea right now. They tell me there were four here last week, but the others have gone on up the Chilkoot trail."

Marianne stared at the sourdough and at the crock containing the sourdough starter. Some gift! She would have to get the bread into the oven. After it rose twice. ... Well, she might as well get busy.

Chapter 6
SOURDOUGH

arianne carefully stoked the fire and got out
the sheet metal oven Thomas had made
from a discarded kerosene can before they
left Seattle. She had been impressed when Thomas
cut out one side of the can and hinged the cutout
piece to make a door for the oven. Now she set the
oven beside the soup over the other hole in their
collapsible sheet iron stove.

"The three Bs," she muttered to herself. "Bacon,
beans and bread. It looks like that's what we'll be
eating. What I wouldn't give for a fresh tomato or a
green pepper."

By the time Thomas returned with the water
jugs he had gone to fill, the dough had doubled in
size, and Marianne was kneading it.

"What's that?" Thomas asked.

"Sourdough," she said. "And that's sourdough
starter," she added, pointing to the crock on the
crate. "Doc gave it to us."

"I've heard sourdough bread is the most practical and popular food for prospectors," Thomas said.
"I can't wait to taste it."

"Well, you'll have to wait until it's done,"
Marianne said. "Would you bring some more wood

for the fire?"

Thomas nodded and headed off to scrounge brush for the fire. Marianne tasted the soup and searched for the jar of Grandma's raspberry preserves she had packed for a special occasion.

This *was* a special occasion, Marianne thought later as she popped the dough into the oven. We've made it this far, and I'm baking my first sourdough bread.

By the time the bread was done, Thomas had returned with a second load of wood. They sat down to enjoy their bread and soup.

"Hey, this looks great!" Thomas spooned raspberry jam onto a slice of the golden brown bread. He took a bite. "You're a good cook!"

Marianne beamed as she helped herself to a slice. The crunchy crust and tangy flavor of the bread were perfect companions for the luscious jam, which reminded them of Grandma and home.

As they were cleaning up after supper, Doc returned. After he accepted the bowl of soup and hunk of homemade bread Marianne offered, he said, "I've been meaning to ask you kids something. What are you doing traveling alone?"

"Our Ma died of consumption two years ago," Thomas explained. "Then last year Pa went off to hunt for gold in the Yukon."

"We stayed with Grandma and helped her run the general store," Marianne added. "Business was just beginning to pick up with all the folks going to the gold fields needing supplies. But then Grandma died, and we were alone."

"But how were you able to finance this trip?" Doc asked as he helped himself to more of the sourdough bread.

"We emptied the cash register after Grandma's funeral; but after buying Marianne's steamship ticket, there wasn't much left," Thomas said.

Marianne scowled at Thomas and added, "But we did bring all the food we could carry from the store. I'm glad for that. At least we can eat even if we don't have much money. We may even have some food to trade for other things."

"We're lucky to have extra food," Thomas said. "Maybe we can open a grocery store."

Doc smiled and asked, "But what about your father? Have you heard from him? Do you know where he is?"

"Last summer Pa wrote us he had reached Fortymile," Thomas explained. "He told us he took the Chilkoot Trail from Dyea. And a boat from Lake Bennett."

"Was he traveling alone?" Doc asked.

"He started out alone, but in Dyea he hooked up with a man named Dusty," Thomas said. "They built a boat at Bennett and floated across the lake and down the river to Fortymile, where they staked a claim. That's the last we heard from him."

Doc shook his head. "I have to hand it to you two, striking out by yourselves. But aren't there folks at home who will miss you?"

Marianne shook her head. "Only Sarah, my friend. She cried with me when Grandma died and again when we learned we would have to close the store."

Gradually Marianne and Thomas had understood why Papa had been so eager to go to the gold fields. It wasn't that he wanted to leave his family. He'd been trying to earn enough money to save the store.

"Sarah's mother would have tried to talk us out of going," Marianne said. "So when I told Sarah we were going north to try to find Papa, I made her promise not to tell anyone—not even her mother—until the day after we left. I told Sarah I'd write to her.

"I'm sorry about your grandmother," Doc said. "You kids really are alone, but stick with me. We'll find your Dad."

Marianne wondered if Doc really could help them?

Later that evening she selected a sheet of lavender note paper from the stationery box she had brought with her and wrote:

Dyea, September 7, 1897
   Dear Sarah,
   I miss you. I wish you were here. But, no, I shouldn't wish this on anyone. I hear there are forty saloons here, and everybody seems to do just what they like. I haven't seen any policemen. It's cold and muddy. Nobody takes a bath; we have to carry water and put it in the washbowl. I sponge off, but what I wouldn't give for a nice hot tub bath!
   I baked my first sourdough bread today. Remember the biscuits Grandma made? And to think we always had plenty of jam and honey to put on them. I miss Grandma's sauerkraut, pickled beets and applesauce, too.
   When you write, could you please slip a comb into the envelope? Mine is losing its teeth.
                        Love, Marianne

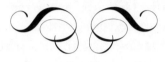
The next morning, Marianne looked for a place to mail her letter. Finally, she gave up, folded the envelope, put it into her pocket, and continued walking along the rows of tents. A town made of tents, tents of all sizes, and no mailboxes, she thought. And mud. Her new Seattle boots were splattered with mud.

Lots of people, but no girls her age, Marianne observed as she headed back to her own tent. Three tents away, she noticed a woman nailing a hand-lettered sign to a tree in front of a tent: *APPLE PIE and COFFEE 25 cents. HOT SOUP 15 cents. Bring your own cup and plate.*

As soon as the sign was up, people rushed to the tent. In no time a line stretched as long as a city block. Marianne looked on in amazement as men stood gulping down the hot soup. Some went back for pie and coffee. The scruffy-looking men were unshaven and dirty. Obviously, they, like Marianne, hadn't eaten a decent meal—or had a bath—in weeks. Marianne closed her eyes and could almost taste the chicken and dumplings and the fruit pies Grandma used to make each Sunday. Even when times were tough, as Papa used to say, Grandma still

managed to come up with Sunday dinner. Marianne
wished she had a quarter to spare for a piece of pie.
I need to get a job, she mused. Everything is so
expensive.

Watching the line moving slowly, Marianne had
an idea. She edged her way to the tent entrance. A
makeshift table served as a work area. Crates and
boxes containing spices, herbs and other foodstuff
were scattered throughout the space. An old gray
blanket hung behind the work area. Marianne
supposed sleeping space was beyond it.

Mustering her courage, in spite of her shaking
knees, Marianne inquired, "May I help you?"

The tall young woman who was running the
restaurant cocked her head, squinted, and peered at
Marianne. "Who are you, and where did you come
from?" Her voice, though harried, was friendly.
Strands of hair straggled down from her bun. Her
long brown corduroy skirt was spattered with flour.

Marianne took a deep breath. "My name is
Marianne Carson. I came to Dyea on the steamer
from Seattle. My brother and I are going to Dawson
City to look for my father, but I need to earn some
money. I could help you." She hesitated. She didn't
want to admit how much she wanted a piece of pie
right now. "We're camped just three tents away." She
stared at the pies in front of her.

The woman looked hard at Marianne. Then she
smiled and extended her hand.

"My name is Johanna Jordan. I can't cook while
I'm waiting on customers. If you want to work with
me, I'll pay you 50 cents a day, and you can have all
the pie you want. If that suits you, you're hired."

"Oh, yes," Marianne said. "That would be fine."

Johanna handed Marianne a ladle. "You can

start by dishing up soup. The customers put their money in that jug beside the kettle. I'll cut pies and get more coffee started. Careful, the soup is hot."

She had a job! A real job! Marianne rolled up her sleeves and began dipping the soup into whatever bowl, cup, or pan each man produced. She noticed some of the men were dressed in rumpled business suits with vests and ties. Others wore bib overalls with oatmeal-colored underwear showing from beneath the straps. A few topped their outfits with cardigan sweaters like Papa had worn when he taught school.

As the men came through the line, Marianne asked several if they knew Robert Carson. No one could remember meeting anyone by that name.

"What's a young girl like you doing up here?" asked a man in a beat-up brown leather jacket and green corduroy jodhpurs. His eyes were bloodshot, his hair unkempt, and he smelled of alcohol.

"I'm going to look for my pa in Dawson City," Marianne said.

"What's your pa's name?"

She hesitated; she didn't like the looks of this man, but maybe he could give her some information.

"Carson. Robert Carson. Do you know him? Have you seen him?"

The man looked away.

"Please, do you know him?"

He looked back at her. "There's ten thousand men running around here," he snapped. "Can't expect to know them all." He hurried away.

Of course it wasn't likely she'd find a man who knew Papa immediately, she thought; but it was strange the way the man had looked away when she mentioned her pa's name.

Marianne kept on ladling soup. Johanna's customers looked tired and dirty, but none appeared too tired to talk. Marianne listened to their chatter.

"My gear's all wet," one man said, tugging at his red suspenders. "The tide came in before I could get my outfit off the beach. I managed to save the boxes, but my flour is paste. I'm glad my rice and coffee were in tins. Then there's that horse I bought in Seattle. I don't know how I'll get her over the trail."

"You don't want to take horses on the Chilkoot," said a man who wore a big hat. "If you have horses, you'd do better to go to Skagway and take the White Pass Trail from there."

"I thought horses were going over the White Pass Trail easily, but now I'm hearing about a lot of dead horses," another said.

Dead horses? As she dished endless bowls of soup, Marianne pictured a trail littered with dead horses. Imagining the stench, she thought she might keel over. She remembered coming upon a dead dog once in a Seattle alley.

She tried to concentrate on what she was doing. It seemed to her that she had been working for hours; but hungry men kept coming, holding out their cups and bowls, dropping their money into the jug. She was hungry, too. She wondered what was done with the dead horses. She was glad there was no meat in this soup.

"Marianne, I've been looking all over for you." She looked up to see Thomas rushing to the tent, out of breath, his face flushed.

She'd forgotten to let her brother know where she was.

"I'd still be looking for you, except someone said a young girl was dipping soup here."

"Oh, Thomas. I'm sorry. I guess I just didn't think."

"We have to stick together," Thomas said. "We don't know anything about all these strangers. Now listen, Doc Elliott will let me go up the trail with him. He has been traveling alone, and he'll need help to build a boat. He has plans and tools. You were right, Marianne. He knows boat building and piloting. We have plenty of food, so we'll make a good team. Doc and I'll start up the trail tomorrow morning before daybreak. We'll return by evening, so we won't have to carry sleeping gear. You stay here."

"Stay here? Alone? But you just said we have to stick together. Now you're going up the trail without me." Marianne's stomach twisted. "What if you don't come back? You will want to, of course, but what if you can't? Papa surely wanted to come back, but he hasn't yet."

"You worry too much, Marianne," Thomas said. "We'll check out the trail. We'll carry our outfits to Canyon City, about eight miles up the trail. Then we'll move everything in batches to the other camps until we reach the summit. You can come with us when we take the last loads."

"Why wasn't I in on this planning?" Marianne wanted to know.

"We didn't know where you were."

Marianne had to admit that was true. "All right. I'll stay here and help Mrs. Jordan."

"Who?"

"Mrs. Jordan. The restaurant lady."

Thomas hesitated, looking around the tent where planks were laid over sawhorses. "I don't know. This doesn't look like a restaurant to me."

"She's a nice lady, Thomas." Marianne said.

"I'm a respectable woman. I'll take good care of her," said Johanna, coming out from behind the blanket that separated the restaurant from her sleeping quarters. "You can see I need help. Working here will be easier for Marianne than trudging up and down that trail."

She introduced herself, and she and Thomas shook hands.

"I'll learn to make apple pie and some special soups," Marianne said. "Then I can make them for you and Doc Elliott. Mrs. Jordan will pay me fifty cents a day."

"Well," Thomas said, "we sure can use the money." He studied the restaurant and Mrs. Jordan. Finally appearing to be satisfied Marianne would be in good hands, he excused himself to return to the tent to start packing.

Later that day as Marianne prepared to head back to her own tent, Mrs. Jordan said, "You're doing a good job, Marianne. You're a good worker. I'm glad to have you helping me. Now get some rest. I'll see you at six in the morning."

Six o'clock! Marianne wanted to tell her that her feet hurt, her arms ached and she was so tired. Instead she said, "Sure, I'll be here."

As she reached her tent and prepared for bed, her mind drifted back to Papa. She remembered the day he had called Thomas and her to his study.

"I'm heading for Fortymile, a Yukon River town," he said. "There's gold to be had there. Thomas, you take care of Marianne, and I'm asking you both to help your grandma. I'll write you."

Papa's first letter confirmed he was settled near Dawson City, but they hadn't heard from him for more than a year. And now they might miss his letter. Or maybe there was no way for Papa to send one out. Perhaps he was sick. Maybe he had written, and the letter hadn't been delivered.

Before she settled down for the night, Marianne wrote another letter, even though she still wasn't sure where or how she could mail it.

Dyea - September 8, 1897
Dear Sarah,

How are things in Seattle? I'm well, but we haven't found Papa yet. I'm selling soup, pie and coffee to hungry men for Mrs. Jordan, the owner of a restaurant tent. Mrs. Jordan makes dozens of pies every day. I think she bakes all night.

Thomas and Doc Elliott, a man we met on the ship, will carry our goods to Canyon City about eight miles up the trail. Then we'll move them little by little to the other camps until we reach the summit. I'm not looking forward to the trail. Thomas and I have been asking everyone we meet if they've seen Papa, but so far no one has.

We haven't received any mail here yet. I wish I could tell you where to write, but we won't be any place very long. I miss you and I think I'm even going to miss school. Finally, I would have been in seventh grade. Isn't this the year we were going to collect leaves and dissect a frog?

Love, Marianne

Chapter 8
DUSTY
September 9, 1897

Marianne handed bags of dried apples and prunes to Thomas as he arranged their belongings in piles.

"They'll taste great with oatmeal," she said. "How much will each of these stacks weigh?"

"Doc said I should put them in piles of forty pounds each," Thomas said as he set down two bags of beans, a slab of bacon, a large sack of rolled oats and a smaller bag of corn meal. He labeled each package CARSON. As he put a huge wheel of cheese beside a bag of dried potatoes, the man with a worn leather jacket and corduroy jodhpurs stopped to watch.

"Pretty big load for a young fellow like you, isn't it?" he said.

"I can manage."

"Lots of folks coming back with no gold. No claims left. Folks are starving up there."

"I guess I'll see for myself."

The man eyed the supplies greedily. "Might better take all that grub and open a grocery store here," he said, spitting a stream of tobacco juice.

"I've got to find my pa. Have you heard of Robert Carson?"

"Nope, never heard of him."

Marianne thought he answered too quickly. The man lowered his head and looked the other way. "But I sure wouldn't be going up that trail if I was you." He wiped his forehead with a dirty red kerchief.

"Well, well, if it isn't old Dusty Olsen. What do you say, Dusty?" The prospector slapped the man on the back.

Marianne noticed the man called Dusty was suddenly in a big hurry to get away. He disappeared among the tents without another word.

"Wasn't *Dusty* the name of Papa's partner?" she whispered to Thomas as soon as the man was gone.

"Yeah, but that man said he never heard of Papa."

"He's lying. Maybe he killed Papa and stole his gold."

"Marianne, stop imagining trouble. There's probably more than one man named Dusty up here. And we don't even know if Papa *found* any gold."

"I don't like the way that Dusty man looked when you asked him about Papa."

Just then Doc appeared with a saw, several lengths of rope and a cask of pitch to be added to the growing pile of goods to be taken up the trail.

"We'll lash the bags and crates onto these wooden pack frames," Doc said.

Seeing Marianne's letters lying on one of the crates, he said, "Shall I take them to the post office? I've a letter of my own to mail."

"I didn't know there was a post office," Marianne said. "I couldn't find a mail box." She handed the letters to Doc.

"Healy and Wilson have a post office inside their

store," Doc said. "The storekeepers will put the mail on the next ship to leave the harbor."

"I need stamps," Marianne said.

"I'll take care of that," Doc said, putting the letters in his pocket.

"Thank you," Marianne said. "I gotta get back to the restaurant now. Let me know when you're ready to leave, so I can see you off."

Later that morning, as she watched Thomas and Doc start up the trail with heavy packs strapped against their backs, her stomach knotted up once more. Here I am separated from Thomas again, she thought. They said they'd be back late tonight, but what if they aren't?

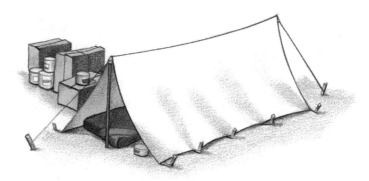

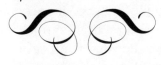

Marianne huddled in her tent, trying to keep warm in the new canvas bedroll Johanna had helped her to sew together.

Having worked all day in the restaurant tent, she was tired; but she tossed and turned. At last, she rose and flung the canvas aside. Wrapping the cape around herself, she crept outside and looked at the stars. Darkness came earlier every night—and it was colder. She shivered. The past two days Doc and Thomas had shuttled goods up the trail, always returning by six o'clock. Tonight it was nearly nine o'clock and there was no sign of them.

Each night when Thomas and Doc returned from Canyon City, they plopped down exhausted on their mats, each in his own tent, without stopping to eat. Later, they'd wake up hungry. After she'd worked all day, Marianne, too, was exhausted, but she'd rustle up bean soup, baked beans or stewed lima beans. But now, she prayed, "Please God, let Thomas and Doc be safe, and I won't complain ever again about cooking for them."

Finally, she went back inside the tent, but still she could not sleep.

The night dragged. Several times she peeked

outside, but she neither saw nor heard anything.

She had just dozed off when voices awakened her. As she opened the tent flap, men appeared carrying someone on a blanket rolled around poles. She froze. It was her brother! She held her breath as Doc and the men pushed into the tent.

"Thomas has a fever," Doc said. "We have to keep him warm. Put that blanket over him."

"Oh, Thomas!" Marianne cried. He looked so gray and lifeless.

"He needs something warm to drink," Doc said.

Marianne felt Thomas's forehead. He was burning with fever, yet he shivered. She rubbed his hands and then hurried to put more wood on the fire and sprinkle tea into the blue granite enameled teapot. She would make the tea nourishing, with lots of canned milk and sugar. After helping Doc pile more blankets on top of Thomas, she poured boiling water over the tea.

When the tea had steeped, she put a tin cupful to Thomas's mouth. Raising his head, he tried to drink it. Coughing and sputtering, he finally swallowed a bit, and then rolled his head back down onto the pillow.

Doc looked around at the fire and the teapot.

"You're doing all the right things, Marianne," he said. "When he finishes his tea, it would be good if you could sponge him with cool water."

"Will he be all right?" Marianne whispered.

"I think so," Doc said. "Thomas was exhausted, so he was an easy target for the fever."

"Are you really a doctor?" Marianne asked. He had said he was, but with Thomas really ill, she wanted to be sure.

Doc paused a moment. He mouth twitched,

and he rubbed his beard. Finally he nodded and said, "Sometimes." He started to leave, but then turned and said, "I'll drop back tomorrow. Meanwhile, keep him warm."

Was he or wasn't he a doctor? As she sat beside Thomas and sponged his forehead while he slept, she still sensed he was burning with fever. After a time, Thomas stirred and babbled in his sleep.

"No, no. Don't, don't. I can carry it myself," he moaned. Then he was still.

As she continued to sponge his forehead, Marianne whispered a silent prayer: "Please let Thomas be all right." Before she left Seattle, she had believed she wanted to be a teacher like Papa. Earlier this week she had considered opening a restaurant. Tonight she thought if she were a doctor, she could help Thomas get well.

If Mama and Grandma were here, they could sit by me the way they used to; and they could help take care of Thomas, Marianne mused.

Her brother stirred again. "It's okay. I can carry it. No, I'm not thirsty."

Thomas thrashed about most of the night, while Marianne continued to watch him with fear and concern. In the morning she hurried to tell Johanna she would not be at work that day.

Arriving at the restaurant tent, Marianne saw a crate full of fresh oranges. A rare treat!

"I'll give you a dollar for one orange," one man was saying.

Another said, "I'll give you two dollars."

Marianne realized men were trying to outbid one another to buy them.

"Oranges! May I take some to Thomas?" she asked Johanna. He has the fever."

"Of course."

Ignoring the protests of her customers, Johanna quickly selected half a dozen and put them in a small basket. As Marianne rummaged in her pocket to find coins, Johanna said, "Put your money away. I hope the oranges will help your brother feel better."

"I'm sorry I won't be able to work today. I hope that won't be a problem."

"Marianne, you take care of your brother. I'll manage. And do let me know how he's doing."

As she ran back to her tent, Marianne stumbled and fell over a box in the middle of the roadway. "These men leave their stuff everywhere," she grumbled aloud.

Scrambling to gather the oranges and brush the mud off her skirt, Marianne looked up to face a girl about her own age. The girl's black braids glistened; a striped woven shawl was draped over a colorful print dress. Her dark eyes and high cheekbones were prominent. She must be one of the native people I've been hearing about, Marianne thought.

"May I help you?" the girl asked.

"No, thanks. I'm fine. Just a little dirty."

"Can I get you something?" the girl asked.

"Thank you. I'll be all right."

"You don't look all right. Are you sure I can't help you?"

"My brother is ill. He has a fever. His head is very warm, and he doesn't talk sense now."

The girl nodded as though she understood. "Many have the fever. Maybe I can help. My mother gathers herbs. I will bring some. They may help your brother."

Herbs? Marianne hesitated. Then she thought, why not? Mama would help if she were here, but she isn't here. Thomas is all I have. "Yes, yes, bring herbs, medicine, —anything. Our tent is the third one beyond the food tent. My name is Marianne. What is yours?"

"Nauk-y-stih."

Marianne looked puzzled.

"It means cinnamon bear."

Marianne tried to repeat the name to herself.

"But I am called Rebecca now," the Native girl said. "The missionaries gave me this name." She held her head high. "I will return soon." She slipped away silently through the row of tents.

The girl seemed a bit aloof, but friendly, Marianne thought. She hurried back to Thomas. Maybe Rebecca could help him, and maybe she would be a friend. Marianne had seen no other girls of her own age in Dyea.

Thomas continued to sleep, but he tossed fitfully.

Rebecca soon returned carrying a small berry basket. The scent of dried herbs was pungent, yet pleasant.

"Put more more wood on the fire, Marianne." The Native girl mixed herbs slowly, but deliberately. When the water was boiling, she put the herbs in a small pan and poured hot water from the teakettle over them. A mint aroma escaped. Like mint tea Marianne's Grandmother used to make.

"Where did you learn to do this?" Marianne asked.

"From my grandmother. She takes care of our people when they are ill. My family are Chilkoot Tlingit, and we carry packs on the trail for the stampeders," Rebecca said as she worked.

"Stampeders?" Marianne questioned.

"The men who hurry here to find gold. Many stampeders have arrived. They all want gold, and they want it right now."

"My father went to find gold last year, " Marianne confessed. "We know he followed the Chilkoot Trail, so my brother and I are going that way to look for him."

"Our clan has been using the Chilkoot Trail for many generations," Rebecca said. "We trade for copper and for moose and caribou hides brought out by interior people. The Tagish and Tutshone also bring beaver, lynx and fox furs."

"What kinds of things do you trade?"

"Blankets, cedar boxes, spruce root baskets, dried fish, eulachon grease and...."

"Eulachon?" Marianne asked. "What's that?"

"Small fish. We call them candlefish. They have so much oil that when dried, they burn easily and provide good light."

Marianne listened, fascinated. To the Natives, many of these items might be more valuable than gold.

When Thomas stirred again, Rebecca brought the herbs near him and let him breathe in the steam.

Marianne hoped she was doing the right thing and wondered if Doc would approve of the herbs. She hadn't seen him yet that day. She would have to do what she thought best.

Finally, Thomas opened his eyes and coughed. Quickly, Marianne pushed an empty pan in front of him. He spit up poisons that had accumulated in his chest and then dropped his head back on the pillow.

The two girls sat silently with Thomas. Occasionally they let him breathe more herbs. Marianne sponged his forehead. His brow was cooler now.

Rebecca looked around the tent. Spying Sophia sitting on Marianne's cot, she exclaimed, "What a lovely doll!"

"Yes, Sophia is special," Marianne said. "She's the only thing I have left that my grandmother gave me. Do you have a doll?"

"Not like this one," Rebecca said. "Our wooden dolls are dressed in bird feathers and animal skins. We decorate them with beads, but your doll wears such fine clothing."

Marianne looked at Sophia. She hadn't thought much about her clothing. Perhaps Sophia was dressed elegantly compared to Rebecca's dolls. Sophia's dress was made of several tiers of white organdy. Her petticoat was trimmed in dainty white lace. Black high button shoes and a white straw hat, banded by a blue ribbon, completed her outfit.

Rebecca rose and turned her attention back to Thomas. "The fever has broken; now he should get well. The herbs are doing their work. Keep him warm. I will return."

"Thank you so much. How much do I owe you for the herbs?" Marianne asked.

"No pay is necessary," Rebecca said. She glanced again at the doll. Then she was gone.

Marianne sat and watched Thomas. He did seem to be breathing more easily. After a while he stirred.

"What am I doing here? How did I get here? I need to get back on the trail," he mumbled. Then he dozed again.

Marianne prayed, "Dear God, don't let him die. Please let him be well soon."

A couple of hours later, he awoke and sat up, flinging aside his blankets. "Where's the rest of our stuff? We have to get it over the pass. Who's watching our gear at Canyon City?"

Is this the way he's supposed to be acting? Marianne swallowed and tried to speak gently, yet firmly. "We'll leave Dyea as soon as you're well, Thomas. Now rest and drink this broth. I have oranges, too."

"Oranges? Where'd you find oranges?" His face brightened.

"A crate of them came in this week's shipment from Seattle. The men were outbidding one another to buy them, but Mrs. Jordon sent some to you. Here, I'll peel one for you."

Doc says oranges, lemons and limes help prevent scurvy," she said as she began to peel the citrus.

Thomas settled back and took the piece of orange offered him. "This tastes good." He bit into a section of orange and sucked the juice. "I thought I saw an Indian girl. Or was I dreaming?"

"You weren't dreaming. That was Rebecca. Her family is Chilkoot Tlingit, and they carry packs on the trail for prospectors who can afford to pay them. She didn't charge for the herbs she fixed for you, though. I'm so glad you're feeling better. You'll be ready to go back on the trail soon, but now you must rest."

In a few minutes Thomas was sleeping again. Marianne put the steaming herbs near him once more and soon was dozing herself.

She was awakened by someone clearing his throat. Marianne looked up to see Doc standing in the doorway of the tent.

As he walked over and placed his hand on Thomas's head, he asked, "How's he doing?"

"Better, I think. He wants to get going, but he's not strong enough yet."

Doc nodded as he checked Thomas's pulse. "You're a good nurse," he said. "Keep him quiet for awhile yet."

"We're losing valuable time, aren't we?" Marianne whispered.

"We're on a tight schedule, but we'll make it."

He didn't sound convincing, and Marianne didn't think he believed it himself.

"Now, I'm off to see other patients. The fever is getting to a number of them. I'll check back soon."

Several hours later Thomas awoke, impatient to

be active again. He sat up and started rummaging through his pack.

"Not so fast," Marianne said. "You've had a bad fever. You need to rest. I know you're eager to get going, but I have an idea. We could hire Rebecca's family to help us carry our stuff over the trail."

Thomas shook his head. "I don't know about that."

"Doc came by while you were sleeping. He says we have to launch our boat at the lake and get on to Dawson City before freeze-up. We've lost time with you being sick."

"I can't help that I was sick."

"I know, but how will we get everything over the summit in time?"

"We'll make it somehow, Marianne, but I don't think we need Rebecca's family to help."

Everything depended on time and money. Marianne was glad she could earn a little money. Grandma had said money wasn't everything; but without it, they would be in serious trouble.

At the store in Seattle Grandma had let many people have groceries on credit. Then, when folks lost their jobs, they hadn't been able to pay up their accounts, so Grandma couldn't make *her* payments. That's why she had lost the store.

Grandma had told Thomas and Marianne they were in the midst of what she called an economic depression. Business was bad, prices fell and people found themselves out of work, she had explained.

Marianne worried about money, and she worried how soon Thomas would be well enough to head over the mountains.

Chapter 11

PARTNERS

September 15, 1897

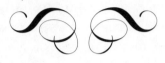

Marianne stayed in the tent three more days, caring for Thomas, feeding him hot soup and tea. As she steamed herbs for him the way Rebecca had taught her, Marianne was torn between her job and Thomas. They needed the money, yet Thomas needed her more. She hoped Johanna would understand and not fire her.

Doc checked on Thomas each evening when he returned from carrying another load up the trail. "He's doing fine," he had assured Marianne the night before. "As soon as he starts eating, we can relax."

On this morning, Thomas sat up and declared he was hungry. After fixing him a bowl of oatmeal and raisins, Marianne told her brother that she must go back to work.

"Mrs. Jordan needs me, and we need the money," she said as she headed for the restaurant tent that rainy morning.

Customers were waiting outside the tent, banging their spoons against their tin plates.

"Hey, here comes our gal. She'll feed us now," one of the stampeders yelled.

"Where have you been, lassie? We've not seen you for several days."

Marianne pushed past them to find Mrs. Jordan in her living quarters tossing tins of spices into a shoebox. Dishes were stacked in a packing crate padded with towels and blankets.

"Whatever are you doing, Mrs. Jordan?"

"Packing, Marianne. How's Thomas? And why don't you call me Johanna? I've made sourdough pancakes for the men. The cakes are under the cloth by the stove. Directions for more are beside the flour sack. Please go and wait on the customers."

"But…"

"Go. I'll talk to you later."

Marianne sighed. She felt left out, but she did as she was told. Reaching the counter, she began dishing up pancakes and carefully rationing the syrup. If she let the men ladle the syrup themselves, it would soon be gone. But she couldn't keep her mind off Johanna. Why was she leaving?

When the morning rush was over, Johanna was at the stove again pouring water over dried potatoes for soup. Marianne waited for an explanation; but after handing Marianne a bag of onions, Johanna went outside without a word.

Marianne selected an onion and began peeling it. Her eyes stung. As she worked, she overheard a conversation.

"Why are you leaving Dyea, Johanna?" Marianne recognized Doc's voice.

"Doc, the men are moving north. I have to go where the business is. I need to set up in Dawson. I've come too far to stop now—much farther from home than I realized."

"Everyone here is a long way from home," Doc said. "Where *did* you come from, Johanna? I've been meaning to ask." Marianne strained to hear her answer.

"From a farm north of Minneapolis. Frank, my husband, wanted to come north to look for gold."

"Where's Frank now?"

"He wanted to be a prospector. I said, 'Fine.' We sold our farm and equipment to outfit him and took a train to Seattle. Frank had had problems before, but he told me he had reformed. He'd quit drinking and gambling, he said. I was a fool to believe him. When we got to Seattle and were waiting for room on a ship, Frank started drinking again and lost most of our grubstake in a poker game. I was so angry I told Frank I didn't want to see him ever again.

"Fortunately, I'd hung on to some money myself so I decided I could make my own way. I learned men up here were living on beans and salt pork. I thought I could provide them with something better. So here I am—cooking."

"And Frank?"

"Dead. I got word he was killed in a shoot-out over a poker game." Marianne heard tears in Johanna's voice.

"I'm sorry." Doc's voice was kind. "Weren't you scared—coming alone to the arctic?"

"I didn't have time to be scared. The ship was sailing. I pulled together as many supplies as I could handle and got on board."

"Do you ever think about going back home?"

"I suppose it crossed my mind, but I... No, I don't want to face Ma and Pa. I don't want to go home and hear Pa say, 'I told you so.' They never did like Frank. I won't be going back to Minnesota, especially now that I've developed a business; but I need to move on up the trail, and I'm not quite sure how I'll manage that."

Forgetting she was eavesdropping, Marianne rushed outside. "Come with us, Johanna!" she said. "A lot of our stuff is already up at Canyon City. Thomas is almost well. We'll have to make about a dozen more trips. Then we'll be ready to move up to the summit."

Marianne held her breath, waiting for Johanna's answer. Johanna looked at Doc, seeking his reaction.

"If I go with you, that will mean another week on the trail for you," Johanna said. "You don't want to haul my gear too."

Marianne was relieved Johanna didn't scold her for eavesdropping.

Doc said, "All you have to haul is your restaurant equipment, food and clothing. You can share our boat, so you won't need lumber and tools. I'd like to have another cook."

"Well—only if I get to be head cook," Johanna said as she smiled and reached for a spoon to stir the soup.

"I'm so glad you'll be coming with us," Marianne said. "Of course you can be head cook."

Later that day Rebecca appeared at the restaurant. "How is Thomas?" she asked.

"Your herbs were just what he needed, Rebecca," Marianne said. "Thomas is ready to travel again. Thank you so much!"

Rebecca was quiet for a long time. She looked around. Finally, she said, "My family can pack your goods over the trail."

"Would they really do that for us?" Marianne asked. "How soon could they get all of our things to the summit? And how much would it cost?"

"I believe the fee is 20 cents a pound," Rebecca answered. "I will ask my family how fast they can

work. If you want them to do the packing, you can
find us at our village down by the river." She pointed
to the north. "Our cabin is just beyond Healy and
Wilson's trading post."

Marianne nodded. She had been at the trading
post looking for supplies one day.

Rebecca left without another word.

She comes and goes so silently, Marianne
thought.

That afternoon Marianne found Thomas up and
about, tying loads onto his wooden pack frame. She
told him about Rebecca's offer and that Johanna
would be joining them.

"Marianne, I don't see how we can hire packers," Thomas said. "Even Doc doesn't have money
for that, and I've heard stories about professional
packers. They're not dependable. Some folks say the
packers drop goods along the trail and carry someone else's if they offer to pay more."

"Rebecca's family wouldn't do that."

"Maybe not, but we'll need all the money we
have to get us through the winter. We'll have to
carry our own packs.

"And I can't imagine Doc wanting to take along
a woman," he added.

"*I'm* a woman… or *almost* a woman," Marianne
retorted.

"But you're my sister," Thomas said.

"Besides, Johanna can help pay for the packing," Marianne said. "She has earned lots of money
with her restaurant, and she'll earn more once we
get to Dawson."

"I don't know."

"Come on, Thomas," Marianne coaxed.

" Johanna has taught me a lot about cooking."

"We'll have to talk with Doc."

"Doc thinks it's a great idea." Then watching Thomas push heavy things around, she asked, "Are you sure you feel well enough to work?"

"Of course," Thomas snapped. "I'm ready to go now." They headed for Doc's tent where they found him lashing together some crates.

"Johanna will be a good addition to our crew," Doc said. "I certainly won't have time to fix meals. Let's get together after supper and make our plans."

That evening as they sat around the campfire outside Johanna's tent, the four discussed their proposed partnership.

"Let's see," Doc began, "what do we want to do when we get to Dawson?"

"We have to find Papa," Thomas and Marianne said in unison.

"I want to operate a restaurant," Johanna said.

"And I've decided to set up a medical practice," Doc said. "Now, what does each of us have to con- tribute to the partnership? I'm a bit short of food, but I can offer medical experience and equipment, and I have everything we need to build a boat— except the lumber."

"I've felled trees and cut firewood back home with Papa, and I can learn how to help you cut planks," Thomas said.

Marianne had seen Thomas using a two-man logger's saw. He was as strong and fast as a man.

"Thomas and I have lots of food we brought from Grandma's store," Marianne offered, uncertain about what else she could contribute to the partner- ship. "I think we should hire Rebecca's family to carry everything. She says the Tlingit have been packing goods over the Chilkoot Pass for years, and they can do it fast, before freeze-up."

"But we can't afford them, Marianne," Thomas repeated. "Besides we've got most of our outfit at Canyon City already."

"True," Doc said, "but the hardest part of the journey is yet to come. Getting over the summit is the most difficult. We have more than two tons of stuff to carry. We could use help."

"But the money!" Thomas protested.

"How much?" Johanna asked. When she learned the cost would be about twenty cents a pound, she did some quick calculations.

"I have enough cash to pay for packing half of our goods to Lake Lindeman," she said.

"I can cover the other half," Doc said.

"Marianne and I can do the cooking, can't we?" Johanna said. "I have brought no boat building materials or lumber, but I can pound nails if you tell me where to hammer. And I'll share my food."

Doc looked at Marianne and Thomas. They nodded.

"You've got yourself a deal." Doc shook Johanna's hand. Turning to Thomas, Doc said, "Let's finish packing."

To Marianne, he said, "Would you find Rebecca and tell her we've a job for her family? If they're available, I'll settle details with their head packer in the morning."

Marianne nodded, proud to have a mission, and took off in the direction of the Tlingit village.

As she walked past her own tent, she noticed a man skulking near their supplies, studying each box carefully. It was Dusty! He turned a bag around so he could see its label, but he edged away casually when he saw Marianne.

That crook was going to steal our food, she
thought. She didn't feel so brave now. She turned
and went back to her own tent. Wrapping her arms
around herself, she sat on her cot shivering. She
knew she ought to tell Doc or Thomas about Dusty;
but they were busy, and her job was to find Rebecca.
She must complete her mission.

Chapter 12
SOPHIA

As Marianne gathered her courage, her eyes fell upon Sophia, there, lying on her cot, as always. The doll was beautiful, she thought, a precious gift from Grandma. She picked up Sophia and held her close. Rebecca had admired her. She would bring her along so Rebecca could see her once more. Carrying Sophia gently, Marianne headed out again to find the packers' headquarters.

Near the riverbank she spotted a cluster of small tents and wooden cabins. This had to be the place. Rebecca had said her family's home was the one nearest Healy and Wilson's trading post. Marianne was relieved to see Rebecca in front of a cabin, but she was surprised at the sign in English above the doorway: "Chief of the Chilkoots." She had not known Rebecca's father was the chief!

After welcoming Marianne, Rebecca said, "My father and his men are busy. Perhaps they will have no time to do any more packing jobs."

Marianne's heart sank. "Of course. Your father is a chief. He must be very busy."

"Yes, we pack for many white men."

Marianne noticed Rebecca was staring at Sophia.

"I see you brought your doll with you," Rebecca said.

Marianne agonized. She loved Sophia. The doll was a reminder of her life in Seattle and her grandmother. Sophia had been her favorite birthday gift from Grandma.

But, taking a deep breath, she held Sophia toward Rebecca. "You helped Thomas get well. You're a good friend. I'm giving her to you."

The girl hesitated, but Marianne nodded. "Please, I want you to have her."

Finally, the Tlingit girl accepted the doll, holding her carefully.

"Thank you," she said. "She's beautiful."

"Her name is Sophia."

"Sophia," repeated Rebecca softly. "That's a lovely name."

"It was my grandmother's name," Marianne said. Although Rebecca still appeared aloof, Marianne believed she would love Sophia.

Rebecca's eyes softened, and she smiled. "I will ask my father again. I will tell him you are my friend."

"Thank you," Marianne said.

Then straightening her shoulders, Rebecca said brusquely, "My family will be at your tent tomorrow morning, early."

Does she have that much power? Marianne wondered; but Rebecca sounded so confident that she could not doubt her. Marianne hurried to tell Doc he could expect the packers the next morning.

Tears slid down her cheeks. Sophia was gone. She had given away the last treasure from her grandmother. But somehow she thought that her grandmother would have approved.

Chapter 13

THE TLINGIT

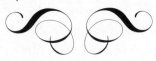

Rebecca arrived with the packers at six o'clock, ready to hit the trail as promised. Marianne noticed the stocky Tlingit men's faces were tanned and weather-beaten. Many wore black mustaches drooping at the ends. Their chests were deep, their shoulders broad. They look as though they can carry heavy loads, Marianne thought.

Rebecca would not be going with them, she told Marianne; but she did want to see them off.

Marianne had carefully nested granite enameled buckets, cutlery and cooking utensils amidst towels and blankets. In a canvas sack, she had stashed boots, oilskin clothing, mosquito netting, heavy underwear and woolen socks. With Johanna's help she had bought some of these things from a restaurant customer who had given up and was selling his outfit at a fraction of what he had paid for it in Seattle.

Johanna had piled her things beside the others. One bag contained flour, cornmeal, oatmeal, rice, beans, sugar, bacon, baking powder and soda.

"What else do you have, Johanna?" Marianne asked.

"Spices, dried fruit, onions and potatoes, coffee, tea and tins of condensed milk. We'll need it all."

Both Johanna and Marianne had hiked up their ankle-length skirts with pins, revealing their bloomers. "Such a nuisance, these bulky skirts," Marianne said. "I wish we could wear trousers like we saw on those women in Dyea."

"Pants would be practical, Marianne; but I think to appear respectable we should keep our skirts for now."

"For now," Marianne said. "But I'm going to get a pair of trousers soon. Skirts are such a bother."

She turned to watch Doc who was strapping and labeling his gear. "Whetstone, hatchet, files, keg of nails, butcher knife, hammer, compass, carpenter's square and canvas tent," he mumbled to himself as he checked them off.

"Two shovels, an ax, three chisels and several other tools are already cached at Canyon City," Doc said when he saw Marianne scrutinizing his goods. "They're all labeled with our names on them."

"Aren't you afraid someone will steal the stuff you left there?" Marianne asked.

"Stampeders look out for one another," Doc said. "Stealing in the North is as serious as murder. If you rob a man of his tools and food, you might as well kill him. He can't survive without them. Don't worry about our stuff. The packers will pick up the gear I left at Canyon City and carry it on for us."

Marianne shuddered and thought again about Dusty who had eyed their food. If he had been Papa's partner, what had happened?

Now she watched as the head packer examined their gear and told Doc what he would charge to carry everything. After considerable shaking and nodding of heads, a deal was made.

Marianne would carry her valise attached to a wooden pack frame Thomas had rigged for her. To save weight, her valise contained only a bottle of water, a change of clothing, her hooded parka and a small amount of food.

"Water is important to prevent dehydration," Doc said. "And don't forget to boil it."

Thomas, Doc and Johanna each bore loads lashed to larger wooden pack frames, but the Tlingit packers would carry the bulk of the goods.

Tlinget pack-straps consisted of two long bands of cotton cloth with a loop at each end. Marianne watched as the loops were fastened to the top and bottom of each load with a small rope and passed around the carrier's shoulders in front. A head strap went over his forehead and was fastened to the load behind. A small blanket under the load served as a cushion.

"This way each packer can carry eighty pounds or more, about twice as much as most stampeders," Doc said.

Some packers wore brightly colored Mackinaw jackets like Doc's. A few wore blue denim jackets. Others wore coats of blanket material. Felt hats, colored kerchiefs or bright wool hats with small rolled brims covered their heads. Marianne noticed each man also carried a stout stick.

"The sticks are for balance and assistance in climbing," Doc said. "I may carry one myself."

The packers wasted no time getting started. Rebecca's father said his crew could transport the entire load in only one trip to Canyon City. From there, the packers would take their goods over the summit and down to Lake Lindeman. As the chief would not be going with them, he bade them fare-well and headed back toward his cabin.

"Let's go," Doc said, as soon as the packers' procession was underway. "We have thirteen miles to hike to Sheep Camp today. Thomas, you set the pace. Marianne, you and Johanna follow. I'll bring up the rear. We'll meet the packers at Lindeman three days from now."

Marianne turned to say good-bye to Rebecca.

"I'll take care of Sophia," Rebecca whispered.

"I'm sure you will," Marianne said as she smiled at Rebecca. "Good-bye for now, and thank you."

Marianne shifted her pack until it felt comfortable. It was time to go.

Chapter 14
THE TRAIL

By mid-morning the sun was high. Marianne's legs and back ached. Her feet were sore. As she struggled with her skirt and tried to adjust her pack, she wondered how she had ever thought she could do this. She'd been on the trail only a couple of hours, and the thought of hiking all day was staggering.

She'd spent a lot of time walking in Seattle with Sarah. Some of the hills in the city were steep, but thirteen miles in one day? Well, she would have to do it. No one was going to hear her complain. "Just put one foot in front of the other," she told herself. She must keep going.

"You could eat an elephant," her grandmother had once said, "if you ate it one bite at a time." Marianne wondered how many bites it would take to eat an elephant. More importantly, how many steps would it take to cover thirteen miles? To distract herself she began counting... twenty-one, twenty-two, twenty-three. ... She'd count to one hundred and then start from one again.

Walk, walk, walk. Forty-one, forty-two. Just keep going, Marianne told herself. ... Seventy-four, seventy-five, seventy-six. ... Along the riverbank, the ground was mostly level, and she could stride along easily. Other times, the path required stepping from rock to rock, which took careful attention and tired her quickly. This time it meant taking off boots and socks and wading through cold, ankle-deep water.

Marianne dried her feet on her skirt, put her boots back on, and set off again. Somehow her aching feet kept moving. "Keep steady. Don't stumble," she whispered to herself.

"I think I've crossed this river five times," she said to Johanna. "Are you sure we're on the right trail?"

"There is only one trail. You're doing all right. Besides, tasks like this build character."

"It ought to help prepare me for a career, eh, Johanna?"

"Sure thing. What kind of work do you think you'd like?"

"When Thomas was sick, I wished I had known more about medicine. I think being a doctor would be great!"

Marianne pressed on with renewed vigor. Gradually she became accustomed to the load, but she felt relieved when Doc said, "Let's stop for a snack here at Finnegan's Point. We're only three miles from Canyon City."

Dozens of tents were scattered beside the river. "All these folks are heading for the gold fields," Doc said. "They don't know anything about the place they're going. They're just going."

"Like us," Marianne thought.

Now she took out chunks of cheese, dried fruit and hard biscuits and laid them on a cloth that Johanna had spread on the ground. Marianne sat down beside the food. It felt so good to rest.

"This is not an easy hike, but you're doing fine, Marianne," Johanna said as she helped herself to a slice of dried pear.

"You women are moving right along," Doc said. "I'm proud of you both." He bit into a chunk of cheese and followed it with a biscuit.

The words were encouraging. Marianne would not disappoint him.

After eating a bite and resting a short time, Marianne's curiosity compelled her to explore. Although she was tired, she didn't want to miss anything. She soon found a blacksmith shop, a restaurant and a tent containing a board lying on sawhorses. A man inside the tent told her he was a bartender, and that the board was his bar. Marianne asked him how Finnegan's Point got its name.

"Dan Finnegan and his sons built up part of the trail and constructed that rickety bridge you crossed a ways back. They've tried charging tolls, but most of the stampeders ignore them."

"Well, we didn't ignore them," Marianne said. It hadn't occurred to her party not to follow the rules. They had paid the dollar each that the toll collectors had demanded, but many of the stampeders obviously weren't as cooperative.

Farther on down the street, a couple of women were running a hotel. A sign on their tent offered a full meal of beans and bacon, bread and butter, peaches and coffee for 75 cents.

"We're moving our cast-iron cooking range up the trail to Sheep Camp and opening a business there," one of the women told Marianne.

"Isn't the stove awfully heavy?" Marianne asked.

"Weighs 200 pounds," the woman said, "but we'll hire packers to move it. The stove will pay for itself in no time."

"They're welcome to that load," Johanna said when Marianne told her about the stove. "My sheet iron stove works just fine."

Then looking around Johanna exclaimed, "What a beautiful place this is! I love the fall colors!"

"I've seen nothing but my feet since we left Dyea, but it *is* beautiful here," Marianne said looking around at the mountains. They towered beyond the stream, beyond the yellow-leafed cottonwoods and weather-beaten sticks and stones.

Marianne picked up a piece of smooth root and ran her hands over the satiny texture. "Look for beauty in small things," her grandmother had told her. Grandma was right, Marianne thought, but suddenly her concentration was broken as streams of stampeders hurried past, some heading for the saloon or restaurant

Doc shook his head. "Many of these fellows don't see the beauty in front of them. They're too busy thinking about the gold."

"I wonder if Papa found any gold," Thomas said.

"Hard to tell," Doc said. "Some people do. Most don't. I saw some folks returning, throwing their gear down beside the trail and heading home empty handed, saying the claims have all been taken. Others say the trail is too difficult, and so they, too, turn around and head back."

Marianne wondered about Papa. He hadn't turned back. But was he well?

"We're right on schedule," Doc added, looking at his pocket watch. Marianne glanced at Johanna and Thomas. No one else appeared tired. Marianne would not admit to being tired either.

"Time to get back on the trail," Doc announced.

"Next stop, Canyon City. Three miles. We'll eat our noon meal there."

And they were off. Marianne sometimes thought her legs would not reach the next foothold as she climbed over jagged boulders and tangled tree roots. But she would not complain. She had been so concerned about her own discomfort today that she had almost forgotten why they were on the trail. They *must* find Papa! Perhaps he was ill. Maybe he needed someone to take care of him and to cook for him. Marianne walked faster.

Canyon City was a welcome sight—a place to rest. Here, beside the Taiya River, they spotted more tents, more muddy streets, and more stampeders, eager to be on their way.

After a meal of canned corned beef, biscuits, dried peaches and lime juice, Marianne was ready to camp, but Doc said it was time to go again. "Only five more miles today," he said. Marianne dragged herself up and prepared for the next leg of the journey. Soon they were slogging through heavy woods, along steep, rocky hillsides. Slippery rocks covered with moss greeted them at almost every turn.

At first Marianne had been embarrassed when she came upon a man nonchalantly relieving himself behind a tree. By now she was getting used to it, but it was with fear and trembling that she stepped off the trail when her own bladder could bear no more. It was impossible to be certain of not being seen. Next time she would ask Johanna to stand guard.

Soon she was back on the trail, walking and counting and stepping from stone to stone. At one crossing Thomas waited for everyone to catch up.

The river bubbled over huge boulders. Previous stampeders had laid a cottonwood log across the rushing water, but to cross on it; they would have to balance carefully, placing one foot directly ahead of the other. Someone had scribbled a sign: *"WATER FIVE FEET DEEP"*

Thomas took the lead. He walked quickly across the river. Johanna went next. She, like Thomas, was sure-footed. Marianne took a deep breath and followed. Stepping gingerly on the narrow log and looking straight ahead at Johanna's back, she repeated to herself, "Don't look down. This log is a bridge twelve feet wide. This bridge is twelve feet wide. This bridge is twelve feet wide."

With a sigh of relief she put her feet on solid ground. Her companions clapped their hands.

"Good job, Marianne!" Johanna said.

"You did great!" Thomas added.

Satisfied to be safely across the river, Marianne glanced back to see Doc, heavier than the others, balancing on the log with his arms outstretched. He started to slip, but miraculously regained his balance. Marianne breathed easier when Doc was on the bank beside them. He wiped his face with his handkerchief.

"Almost got a cold bath there," Doc said. "You kids were fantastic! You're both surefooted as goats." Then they were on the way again.

"Waterfall ahead!" Thomas shouted.

"Wow!" Marianne exclaimed. "It's beautiful!" Water cascaded down the side of the rocky gorge. Golden aspen intermingled with dark green hemlock. Lush ferns covered the ground. Marianne stopped to look.

"Bear tracks!" Thomas shouted.

"Did you say bear tracks?" Marianne asked. "I'd like to *see* a bear, but I don't want to *meet* one." As they moved on, she heard a rustle in the bushes. She froze. A red squirrel scampered through the brush. Marianne relaxed and continued on her way.

When Marianne thought she could go no farther, Thomas called out, " Pleasant Camp!"

Spruce and cottonwood trees provided shade. Golden leaves carpeted the ground. Sparrows chirped and ravens cackled.

"How'd this camp get its name?" Marianne asked.

"Doc told me this is a pleasant respite from the gloomy gorge," Thomas said.

"I didn't think that gorge was so gloomy," Marianne said. "I thought it was beautiful."

"Depends on your point of view, I guess," Thomas said.

In no time Johanna produced a snack. The others crowded around and sat down to enjoy dried apricots and crackers.

"We're only a few hours from Sheep Camp," Doc said. "We'll spend the night there."

After resting and paying another toll to cross one more bridge, they started again. The ground was level now, and Marianne tried to enjoy the scenery. But the muddy ground slowed her. She began counting her steps again.

Chapter 15
SHEEP CAMP

Finally, they reached the day's destination. Sheep Camp was a settlement of hundreds of tents wedged together so closely that there was barely space for a person to squeeze between them. The camp was a bedlam of sweating men and yelping dogs. Starving horses hobbled about the camp, their backs raw from heavy packs and their legs cut and bruised by rocks.

Marianne noticed a tent with a sign advertising *"LETTERS CARRIED TO DYEA FOR 10 CENTS"* She hesitated; then she decided it would be worth it. She would write to Sarah tonight.

"Hey, there's a hotel here," Thomas said. A huge cloth sign on the front of one of the two wooden buildings in town proclaimed HOTEL. Thomas hurried to explore, returning shortly with the announcement that meals were 75 cents per person and that there was no charge for sleeping privileges.

"We just lay our blankets anywhere we can find a place," Thomas said.

"I suggest we sleep in our own tents and prepare our own food," Johanna said.

"Drat, I thought we wouldn't have to set up tents tonight. Why can't we stay in the hotel?"

"I like the privacy of my own tent; and our food is not only better, it's already paid for," Johanna said.

"But it's work to set up these tents," Thomas grumbled to Marianne.

"I think we should listen to Johanna," Marianne said.

"Women," he mumbled as he prepared to make a fire.

"Marianne, can you find a package of dried potatoes in that pack and set water to boil, please?" Johanna directed, as Doc and she laid tarps and set up the tents.

"This place used to serve as headquarters for hunters looking for mountain sheep," Doc said.

"I think sheep are the only creatures that could cling to some of these cliffs," Johanna said.

Marianne gulped. Tomorrow they would climb near those cliffs to the summit. She took off her boots and rubbed her feet.

Seeing Marianne grimacing, Doc offered corn and bunion plasters. "Put these on your feet each morning and that should relieve the pain," he said.

Gratefully Marianne accepted the plasters. He never stops being a doctor as well as being a good hiker and adventurer, she thought.

"Sheep Camp looks as though it could use another restaurant," Johanna remarked. "We could make good money. There must be as many folks here as in Dyea."

"No time," Doc said. "We've got to keep moving. We need to get over the summit, reach Lindeman, build our boat and get down the river to Dawson City before the ice sets up, or we'll spend the whole winter in Bennett."

"You've convinced *me*," Johanna said. "I'll be up

at dawn, ready to go."

Although Marianne could not remember ever having been this tired, she didn't want to spend the winter on the trail. She, too, would be ready to go at dawn.

After their evening meal of sourdough biscuits and potato soup seasoned with bacon, Marianne helped with clean up and then headed off to explore the camp. She walked along the dirt path that appeared to be the main street of the town.

Men and women were hanging laundry on bushes, frying bacon over open fires and baking bread in makeshift ovens. They smiled at Marianne. "You're a long way from home for such a young one," one of the women said. "Come have a bite to eat."

Marianne shook her head, "No thank you," she said and hurried back to her own camp. She wanted to write to Sarah.

September 16, 1897
Dear Sarah,

We have reached Sheep Camp, named this because sheep hunters used to camp here. Now it's a stopping-off place for stampeders—the people who have come to look for gold—before they head over the summit. Tomorrow we'll climb there, too.

This will be the most difficult part of the trip, and we could run into snow near the top of the mountain, but after the summit, it will be mostly downhill. The packers we hired are already far ahead of us. They'll leave our outfits at Lake Lindeman. We'll travel from there by water. I'm eager to be at the lake where I'll help build our boat.

I miss you. I think about you in school. What

*books are you reading? Do write and tell me what
is happening in Seattle. We've not seen a newspaper since we left Dyea. We're traveling with
Johanna who was running a restaurant in Dyea,
and Doc, the doctor who helped us unload our
goods at Dyea. Doc said you can send a letter to
me at Dawson City, Yukon Territory, Canada.
Mark "HOLD" on the envelope.*

Love, Marianne

She hoped Thomas wouldn't be upset that she
was spending a whole dime on a letter. After deliver-
ing her note to the "post office" tent, Marianne went
back to her own tent and looked up at the stars.
They seemed much brighter here than in Seattle.

Suddenly white lights shimmered and danced in
the northern sky, like skirts swishing. The Aurora
Borealis, her grandmother had called them.
Marianne had watched the Northern Lights from
Seattle, but the colors had never been like this.
Golden, green, blue and purple lights flashed over-
head, pulsing and shifting. They are so incredibly
beautiful, Marianne thought.

After watching the show for some time,
Marianne crawled into her tent and was asleep
within seconds, dreaming of girls wearing colorful
gowns, dancing at a holiday ball in Seattle. Or were
they waltzing in Dawson City?

Chapter 16

THE CLIMB

Next morning Doc prepared a hearty breakfast of sourdough pancakes and bacon. "It's time the cooks had a rest," he said.

Although Johanna protested they should be conserving food, Doc said, "We have to keep up our strength."

"Yeah," agreed Thomas. "These sure are good, Doc. We may make you chief cook."

Marianne and Johanna exchanged glances.

After the feast and clean up, they headed for the Chilkoot Pass.

"The first part of this trek is called *Long Hill*," Doc explained.

For good reason, Marianne thought as the trail rose steadily.

"That huge glacier on the side of the mountain. looks as though it could fall right off the side," Thomas said. Jutting over and downward was a mass of ice.

"It could fall on us," Marianne said.

"It's a mile away," Thomas said. "You worry too much."

After a time, the group rested in a rocky, level place and prepared to tackle the steep climb ahead.

"It's not as steep as it looks," Thomas said, "but it *is* almost a 45-degree angle to the top."

"They call this area *The Scales*," Doc explained. "A fellow at Sheep Camp told me it gets its name because packers often weigh their loads again here before continuing to the summit. We were warned that some packers increase the price here."

Thousands of tons of outfits were piled up, waiting for their owners, who had gone back for more of their supplies. Many had stenciled their names with paint on their bags and boxes. Others had attached tags with wire.

Today, the summit was enveloped in mist and clouds, but Marianne could see packers and other climbers ahead. Men in denim and wool trudged up the mountain. They looked like ants scrambling among the rocks.

Suddenly the weather changed from unseasonably warm autumn to early winter. A gust of cold air replaced the balmy breeze. Thick flakes of snow fluttered around. As Marianne stopped to put on her hooded parka, she was glad Doc had helped her and Thomas find warm jackets in Dyea.

Looking back, Marianne thought they might be halfway up already. But the path got rougher. Rocks, from the size of a bread box to boulders the size of an icebox, obstructed the narrow, winding footpath. At times, Marianne crawled on hands and knees from boulder to boulder, careful not to lose her footing on the smaller loose rocks. She stopped to catch her breath and shift her pack.

"Keep moving!" someone shouted from behind. Half a dozen stampeders closed in upon her.

"Can't they see I'm only twelve years old?" Marianne muttered to herself.

"Relax. Take your time." Doc's calm voice was reassuring.

Marianne let the impatient stampeders pass. Why was anyone trying to conquer this land? They say they want gold, but is the gold worth it? She wondered if the *possibility* of gold was worth it? Taking a deep breath, she hiked up her skirt again and reminded herself why *she* was here: Papa.

Again she started counting her steps. Somehow counting made the trek bearable; yet she could scarcely see where she was going, the mist was so thick. She followed Thomas closely. Johanna and Doc followed her.

The mist grew denser, and snowflakes appeared on Marianne's parka. The thought of tromping through snow on this, the most treacherous part of their journey, was terrifying. She concentrated on her destination, but never had she felt so close to giving up. She was so tired

"I'm going to look for Papa," she said aloud. "I don't care if he found gold or not. I just want to find him and take him home. I want for us all to go home."

Home, she thought. But where is home now? Grandma's gone. The store's gone. Was Seattle really home now? Would Papa ever want to return there?

"You're doing fine, gal," Doc encouraged as he came up close behind her. "It won't be much farther."

After three grueling hours, they reached the summit. The rocky trail was covered with a dusting of fresh snow, but the mist had cleared.

"Look, we can see forever!" Thomas yelled.

Reaching his side, Marianne saw that indeed she could see for many miles. She forgot her aches and pains. A panorama of mountains surrounded her. Looking down into the valley, she saw a body of pure blue water ahead. Her skin tingled. Wow! This was really something. She felt like she was part of the whole universe. She had really climbed this mountain. If she could do that, she could do anything. She would remember this moment forever.

She clapped her hands and hugged Thomas. "Isn't this wonderful?"

"It sure is, Marianne. It's great!"

"Crater Lake," Doc said as he hurried beside them. "How lucky to have a clear day. I've heard it's often so cloudy up here you can't even see the lake."

Marianne hugged Johanna. She hugged Doc. She was so happy to have made it to the summit.

"This is all worth it, isn't it?" Johanna said.

"We've achieved one more milestone," Doc said. "You all are real troopers."

Looking around, they saw other stampeders with their tents, tarps, tools, lumber, live chickens, turkeys and other foodstuffs stacked about. Some men were sledding goods down the sloping snowfield between the summit and Crater Lake.

Marianne and her companions stretched, rested and congratulated themselves that they had come this far in just a day and a half.

"Some folks have to make forty trips before they get all of their outfit across," Doc reminded them.

Marianne was glad she had to make the journey only once. The Tlingit packers already had delivered their goods safely at the summit and would carry them on down to Bennett.

"You were right, Marianne, to insist on the packers," Thomas said.

How lucky I was to meet Rebecca, Marianne thought. Then, remembering Sophia, a lump formed in her throat, but she bit her lip. "I've no time to think about dolls here," she said to herself. "I have to concentrate on not falling off the mountain.

"Couldn't we camp here tonight?" she asked as they snacked on leftover breakfast biscuits.

Doc shook his head. "We're doing fine, but if we're to make it out of Lake Lindeman before freeze-up, we have to keep going. And as you can see, there's no good place to camp here. It's only three miles to Happy Camp."

Three more miles today! Marianne groaned. She wished they didn't have to be in such a hurry. Her muscles ached. Her feet were blistered. But thanks to Doc, she now had corn and bunion plasters to put on her feet each morning. And it looked as though the journey would be downhill from now on.

Marianne awoke to the aroma of hotcakes. Her teeth chattered, and she shivered as she pulled on her clothes. After dressing quickly, she hurried outside.

Here at Happy Camp with the weather clear, she looked back up the trail toward the summit and then ahead toward Lake Lindeman, six miles farther. Either way, she could see a steady line of people dragging or carrying their goods.

Spotting a few wild blueberries, she decided they would taste good on pancakes and proceeded to gather them in her pocket.

As they ate breakfast together, Marianne found the fresh blueberries tangy yet sweet on Johanna's sourdough hotcakes.

"Good hotcakes, Johanna," Marianne said.

"Thanks," Johanna replied. "Doc's sourdough has been a godsend."

"And your blueberries add just the right touch, Marianne," Doc said.

Marianne was glad she had given the sourdough to Johanna for safekeeping. Johanna regularly added flour and water to keep the starter active. I would never remember to do this, Marianne thought. It's all

I can do to keep track of what day it is.

After clean-up, it was time to move on. They put on their packs and headed down the mountain. This will be easy, Marianne thought, but soon she found it more difficult to go down than up. After hiking several hours, her legs were rubbery. Her knees felt as though they were being pounded into her legs.

She dragged her feet, but again she remembered that by putting one foot in front of the other, she would reach her destination.

"I'd like to just lie down and stay here," she said. "My legs don't want to move." It was becoming more and more difficult to keep up with Thomas.

"Let me help," Johanna said. "Lean on my arm."

"No, I'll manage," Marianne protested. Johanna's face was flushed and her hair straggly. Johanna's tired, too, Marianne thought. She couldn't ask her to bear more weight. Stopping to take a drink from her water bottle, Marianne sat on a rock. Johanna joined her.

"It's good that Doc makes us boil drinking water each evening," Johanna said.

Marianne nodded, but thought to herself that sometimes it took so long to build the fire and wait for the water they took from the stream to come to a rolling boil that she had become impatient. So far, though, none of them had become ill from bad water, so probably Doc was right.

"Maybe I'll study medicine," Marianne said, more to herself than to Johanna. "Doc says someone needs to tell people about bacteria and germs. He's trying to do that, but he needs help."

"Doc knows a lot, and he likes to help people," Johanna said. "He told me he had a good practice in

Seattle, but he spent most of his time seeing patients who couldn't afford to pay. He's hoping to strike gold so he won't be as dependent upon income from his medical practice."

"I think I'd like to be a doctor," Marianne said, "but I don't know if I could. There aren't many women doctors."

"You can do anything you set your mind to, my dear," Johanna said.

"But it takes money to go to medical school, and I'm not even in high school yet."

"True, but you can go to school in Dawson. Didn't you tell me your pa's been a teacher? He could teach you if there's no school in town. Maybe he could even start a school."

"I don't know if Papa would want to do that," Marianne protested.

"We don't know that he wouldn't though, do we?"

Johanna rose. Marianne pushed the cork back into the neck of her water bottle and stepped back onto the trail. She would think more about what it would be like to be a doctor. That would make her day go faster. As she trudged along, gradually she forgot about her rubbery legs and fantasized about taking care of sick children and seeing the happiness on their parents' faces when the children recovered. But as she thought about cleaning wounds, she wondered if she would be able to stand the sight of blood.

After what seemed hours of walking, she saw the lake below.

Lindeman was a long lake, colored grayish green by the glacial silt, which had washed down from the ice fields above. Mountains beyond mountains, their tops cloaked in clouds, provided a backdrop for dozens of boats under construction along the shore. As they approached the settlement, Marianne could see men sawing and hammering, hurriedly putting together scows and rafts of many shapes and sizes. Sawdust floated everywhere, but the air was fresh and crisp. Golden willows lined the lakeshore.

"Some of those boats look like cigar boxes with a sail," Thomas said.

"You're right," Doc agreed. "But whether they look like a cigar box or a real boat, each builder hopes his craft will make it through the rapids. He hopes it will carry him and his companions and their outfits across the lake, on through Lake Bennett and down the Yukon River to Dawson City. Now let's look for our belongings."

Doc and Thomas soon found their cache of goods and took a quick inventory. Johanna thanked the Tlingit boss packer who waited impatiently to collect the fee. As soon as she had paid the head-man, the team of packers disappeared silently back up the trail, back to more customers in Dyea.

"Let's pitch our tents here," Thomas suggested. Clusters of scarlet bunchberries with purple-red leaves covered a patch of level ground at the edge of a willow thicket.

"I think we should pitch them over here on higher ground where it will be dryer and safer," Doc said.

Marianne noticed that Thomas agreed without comment. A week ago he might have questioned Doc's decision, but now he readily accepted Doc's leadership.

Following Doc's instructions, they proceeded to set up camp on the higher ground. When the tents were pitched, Johanna and Marianne unpacked flour and bacon while Thomas scrounged for firewood and Doc went to fetch water.

When they returned, Thomas said, "The men are talking about rough rapids between here and Bennett."

"Yup," Doc said. "They're rough, but we can handle them. We'll begin building the boat tomorrow."

The plan, Doc explained, was to build a flat-bottomed boat to carry them and their goods. He pulled sketches from his jacket pocket. "Our scow will be twenty-four feet long, and eight-feet wide at the center. The 26-inch sides will flare, and the stern should be wide and square. She should draw only a foot of water when loaded. We'll rig a square sail from that large canvas tarp I brought."

Thomas looked at the sketches, and Marianne could see he was eager to begin.

"I'm glad you know what to do," Johanna said. "Tell us how to help. Meanwhile, Marianne and I will feed you."

That night Marianne wrote:

Lake Lindeman - September 18, 1897
Dear Sarah,

We've arrived at Lake Lindeman after three days of hiking. The Tlingit packers brought our goods here, and now we're ready to build a boat that will take us across several lakes and down the Yukon River to Dawson City, where we'll look for Papa. I'm glad we didn't have to carry all of our gear ourselves, or we'd still be walking back and forth with many loads.

The lake is magnificent! We'll have great

scenery while we're building our boat.

Have you thought about what you want to do when you grow up? Johanna thinks I could be a doctor if I want to. A doctor has to study a lot of hard things. I hope I do well in science, but I don't even know where or when or if I'll be in school again.

We haven't received any mail yet, but I know you're writing, so I'll be patient. I hope your letters catch up with us in Dawson City.

Love, Marianne

She crawled into her bedroll. The hike was over. In the morning construction would begin. The boat ride might be scary, but riding could not be as tiring as walking. She felt so grimy. Perhaps she could figure out a way to do some laundry in the morning. If she could just find time to wash her hair. ...With these thoughts whirling in her head, she fell asleep.

Chapter 18

BOAT BUILDING

September 19, 1897

Marianne awoke to the sound of sawing. Jumping up, she saw Johanna already had a fire going.

"Good morning," Johanna greeted her. "Did you sleep well?"

"Fine," Marianne answered. "Good morning. But why didn't you wake me?"

"You were especially tired last night and I thought you needed extra rest. You look refreshed now. Let's have breakfast."

"Sounds good," Marianne agreed as she unpacked cereal and dried fruit.

"I'm fixing sourdough biscuits," Johanna said. She set aside a cup of the batter to use as starter for a future batch. "Would you see if you could find that crock of apple butter we've been saving?"

"Where'd you get the tables, Johanna?"

"These are a couple of sawhorses and planks I borrowed from some of the other boat builders."

If Johanna doesn't have what she needs, she always manages to find it somewhere, Marianne thought. "Where are Doc and Thomas?"

"Already up and out cutting logs into boards. Would you find them and tell them breakfast is almost ready?"

Marianne skipped away to look for Doc and her brother. She found them amidst rows of sawpits, all full of busy men and women. Each pit contained a sturdy log frame constructed by the boat builders. On the frame rested the log to be sawed. One person balanced on top of the log, pulling and pushing one end of the long, narrow whipsaw, while another worked the lower end. In this way two people sawed each log into boards.

Marianne stood, mesmerized by the process. Doc and Thomas worked together amiably, she noticed, taking turns at being up and down. One would work in the sawpit while the other worked from above. After several minutes, they exchanged places.

But all twosomes were not so compatible. Marianne heard cursing. One partnership dissolved in front of her eyes.

"You take your stuff and go," yelled a burly man wearing a black plaid mackinaw coat. "My eyes are so full of sawdust, I can't see. Just give me half of that grub."

"You can have all of those goll dang beans," retorted his partner, a tall slim man in a denim jacket and oilskin pants. "I'll take half of the sourdough starter. And leave me the stove."

"I'll give you *half* of this stove. Just you watch." The man in the mackinaw grabbed an ax and began hacking away at the stove.

"Two angels could not use one of these whip-saws without getting into a fight," one of the by-standers said.

Marianne put her hands over her ears and turned her attention to two men in red coats who hurried to break up the argument between the men.

Others in red coats continued to move among the boat builders.

"Make your boat strong and long," one of them advised. "The Yukon is both strong and long. Take your time."

Time. Marianne remembered her errand. She hurried back to Doc and Thomas. "Breakfast is ready," she called to them.

Glad for a recess, they stopped work and followed her.

"Who are the men in the red coats?" Marianne asked.

"North-West Mounted Police," Doc said. "They're here to keep order and to see that most of us survive. They're inspecting and registering each boat."

Looking around, Marianne saw canoes, barges, kayaks, canvas boats and wooden boats. Some looked like packing boxes. Others resembled coffins. Marianne shuddered.

Back at Johanna's kitchen, food was already on the makeshift table. Johanna had set up a sign she had made from a piece of scrap lumber: *COFFEE, SOURDOUGH BISCUITS, APPLE BUTTER AND OATMEAL - 50 CENTS.* She was happily collecting money and ladling oatmeal into bowls as men crowded around the table. Doc and Thomas grabbed bowls, filled them and stood near the table eating.

"Are we opening another restaurant?" Marianne asked. She would feel more comfortable cooking meals than boat building.

"We can use the money to buy lumber," Johanna explained. "I found a man selling boards already cut. We can save at least a week if Doc and Thomas don't have to work that whipsaw."

"I wouldn't object to that," Doc said. "I'll check on the lumber right after breakfast."

The food line continued to form, and the money rolled in.

"Johanna has found her own way of mining for gold," Marianne said.

"You were right to insist we bring her along," Thomas said.

Johanna and Doc exchanged smiles.

"Have you seen my Pa?" Marianne asked the men as they came to get breakfast. "His name is Robert Carson." No one had.

"You can sort these beans," Johanna said, handing her a bag of what she called white navy beans. Take out any stones or black spots you find among the beans."

The beans were white. Why they were called *navy*, Marianne couldn't imagine.

Johanna continued to purchase extra food from those going out who wanted to lighten their loads. She would set up her portable grub tent wherever she could, she told Marianne.

"We'll offer a special bean soup to customers tonight," Johanna said. "Be sure to add plenty of onions and dried parsley to the soup. Toss in a little bacon. We don't want our soup to taste like the slop most of them have been eating since they left home. We'll serve cornbread and maple syrup with the soup. Our meal will be special."

"One thing about you, Johanna," Marianne said, "is that your meals are never boring."

"On their own, most of the stampeders would eat nothing but plain beans and sourdough bread," Johanna said.

As they chopped onions and parsley, Marianne and Johanna chatted.

"I think you'd enjoy the story about Elizabeth Blackwell," Johanna said.

Marianne nodded. She remembered reading a short piece at school about the first woman doctor in the United States. Dr. Blackwell's acceptance into the world of medicine had been difficult, but she had persevered and helped lead the way for other women to enter the field. Marianne hoped there would be a library in Dawson City.

Doc and Thomas returned with some of the lumber Johanna had told them about.

"Now we can concentrate on building a boat instead of sawing logs," Thomas told Marianne. "Thanks to Doc, our craft will be sturdy and water-tight."

That night a rustling in the bushes awakened Marianne. She rose and peeked out of the tent. Someone was rummaging around their cache of supplies. Marianne froze, not sure what to do. If she screamed, she might be attacked. She reached across the tent and nudged Thomas.

"Wake up," she whispered. "Someone is trying to steal our food."

Thomas snatched his gun, crept out of the tent, and cocked the rifle. Marianne held her breath.

Thomas fired into the air. A man yelled and took off running.

"Did you recognize him, Thomas?"

"Looked like that fellow, Dusty—the one we saw in Dyea and again at Sheep Camp."

"I don't like him."

"You worry too much, Marianne."

"How can I not worry?"

Doc and Johanna came crawling out of their separate tents.

"What was that shot all about?" Doc asked.

"Someone was trying to steal our food," Thomas said. "I fired to scare him away."

"Is everyone okay?"

"We're fine," Marianne said. "Just a little shook up." The shot had drawn other stampeders from their tents. Men in long underwear staggered out, rubbing their eyes.

"Everything's under control," Doc told the stampeders. "Go back to bed." Then he turned to Thomas. "Stray bullets can cause havoc."

"That's why I shot up in the air," Thomas said.

"Good thinking," Doc agreed. "I didn't mean to criticize. You kids are incredible."

Next morning Doc and Thomas checked the supplies and boat. Nothing seemed to be missing, they reported. "But where did that scoundrel go?" Doc muttered.

As she was serving breakfast, Marianne listened to the chatter of the men gathered around Johanna's makeshift table.

" . . . bad rapids on that One Mile River between here and Bennett," one said. "Lindeman Rapids, they call it."

"Yup, but nothing like we'll meet up with at White Horse Rapids. White Horse is so dangerous some boatmen are charging a hundred bucks to pilot a boat through."

Marianne caught her breath, but Doc who was just heading out to begin building their boat, said, "We'll handle the rapids ourselves, gal. Don't you fret."

Doc seems so confident, she thought.

"Yes, we'll deal with rough water when we get there," Johanna added. "Maybe we'll even enjoy the ride! Let's get the boat built and not worry about the rapids."

"All right," Marianne said. The hardest part was not knowing what to expect, but as her grandmother had said, "Most things one worries about never happen." But she was worried about Papa. A letter should have caught up with them by now. It was strange none of the folks she'd asked had heard of Papa—except maybe for Dusty.

"What if Dusty has stolen Papa's gold?" Marianne asked Thomas that evening as they prepared for bed. "And *killed* Papa?" What will we do, Thomas?"

"We don't know that any such thing happened, Marianne."

"No, but we don't know that it didn't."

"I thought you weren't going to worry about things you can't control."

"I did say that, didn't I? Well, I'm trying."

Next day Doc put Johanna and Marianne to work caulking the bottom of the boat. "This will prevent the boat from leaking," he explained. "Don't hurry. Just be sure to fill in all of the cracks. You two can work on this while Thomas and I cut boards for passenger seats. We'll also have to select a straight spruce trunk for the mast."

Johanna set a pot of black pitch to boil on the stove.

"This caulking is sticky, smelly and hot," Marianne complained when she saw what their job would be.

"You're right, but it has to be done," Johanna said. "We don't want a leaky boat."

Soon they were dipping stringy fibers of oakum into the pitch. Blisters formed on Marianne's hands as she attempted to hold the hot oakum in place and pound it into the seams between the planks with a hammer and chisel before it cooled.

Caulking was a miserable job, but Marianne was proud when the job was done. She was satisfied their boat would not leak.

Johanna and Marianne then set about making supper.

"Let's have peaches for dessert," Johanna said as she set a can of fruit on the table.

"Where'd you get those?" Marianne asked.

"From a fellow named Josh who has been to Dawson City. That's him in the business suit with a box strapped to his back, talking to Doc. He was carrying six tins of peaches in his pack. No wonder he's heading back to Tacoma. Carrying tin cans across the pass is ridiculous. But his folly is our gain. I got the fruit real cheap. He even threw in some vinegar and baking powder."

Marianne headed toward Doc and Josh so she could hear their conversation.

"The White Horse rapids are about a half-mile long," Josh said. "The dangerous point is at the very foot of them. A rock comes out from the left shore, and the waters boil around it two to five feet high."

Doc scribbled notes as he listened.

"You'll know you've reached Dawson when you see the shape of a moose hide on the mountain," Josh added.

"A moose hide?"

"Yes, the gray scar up on the mountainside is an

unmistakable landmark—left there by a landslide of rock and gravel."

"Thanks for your help." Doc put the notes in his pocket.

"Good luck to you," Josh continued. "I'm going back home where I belong. I'll have to find some other way to get rich. I'm an unemployed newspaper reporter, but now I have plenty to write about. If I can sell my story to a publisher, I'll be in business." He headed down the trail.

Johanna, always trading and bargaining, Marianne thought as she opened the can of peaches. *I hope I can do as well when Thomas and I are on our own. On our own!* She tried to imagine what it would be like for her and Thomas to be on their own. The thought was both exciting and frightening.

Marianne watched Johanna and Doc working confidently, and she recalled her Pa and Grandmother working hard back home. She wondered if grownups ever had time for fun. She remembered tea parties she and Sarah had held with Sophia and their other dolls. Sophia. Well! There would be no more tea parties with dolls.

Chapter 19

CAMPFIRES

❦

T hat evening they chatted around a campfire with other stampeders. One of the men said, "I hear some folks had to turn back because of the flood."

"What flood?" Johanna asked.

"Sheep Camp was wiped out by a mud slide and flood the morning of the 18th," the man explained.

"That's only a day after we camped there," Marianne said.

"How do you know that?" Thomas asked her.

"I've been keeping track of the days."

"I'm impressed, Marianne," Thomas said. Then turning to the stampeder, Thomas asked, "What happened?"

"The glacier ice dam broke. About 7 o'clock in the morning tons of water and rock crashed down from the mountain and poured into the river, washing away tents and outfits. The big saloon tents and many small ones were wiped out. There's nothing left along main street but mud and slush. People were digging out what they could find, wringing out their trousers and underwear. Lots of folks lost everything. Others are selling what's left of their stuff cheap and going back Outside."

Something like that could happen to *us,* Marianne thought. We might have been caught in that mudslide! Or we could capsize the boat at White Horse Rapids.

"Any lives lost?" Doc asked.

"Eighteen missing," the man said. "No report of deaths yet." The man bid Marianne and her party goodnight. *He* was obviously not going to give up.

"We're not giving up either," Marianne said to herself.

After six days of hard work the sturdy scow was finished.

"What a great boat!" Marianne said.

"You men did a good job," Johanna added.

"We couldn't have done it without your money, Johanna," Doc said, "and without you and Marianne helping with meals and with caulking."

"What shall we name it?" Thomas asked.

"What do you suggest?" Doc asked.

"How about Sophia?" Marianne offered.

"After a doll? How silly," Thomas said.

"That was Grandma's name, you know."

"Oh, yes, you're right." Thomas's face reddened. It was almost as though he had forgotten. "Shall we smash a bottle over Sophia's prow?"

"We can't waste any bottles nor their contents," Johanna said.

"I'll just pretend then." Thomas picked up a smooth stick. "I hereby christen you *Sophia.*"

The others clapped.

"Now let's pack up and head for Bennett," Doc said.

"I'm not wearing this bulky skirt any longer," Marianne declared as soon as Doc and Johanna were out of earshot. "Thomas, may I have a pair of your trousers? Those gray tweed ones are too small for you anyway. I think they'd just fit me."

"But, Marianne, only *bad* women wear trousers,"

"Nonsense. I've made up my mind. Skirts are a bother."

Reluctantly, Thomas produced his outgrown trousers, and Marianne went inside the tent to change. She also took the diary and unmailed letters from her valise and placed them in a waterproof tin.

Marianne felt strange as she moved about the tent, for she had never worn trousers. How different not to feel the heavy skirts around her legs. The trousers gave her a feeling of freedom because the legs moved with her instead of constraining her.

Doc and Johanna expressed surprise at Marianne's new attire.

"Now don't you look like a young man," Doc said.

Marianne was trying to think of a comeback when Johanna came to her rescue.

"I think her outfit makes a lot of sense. Trousers would have made our hike much easier."

"I suppose you're right," Doc said as he hoisted his pack up on his back. "It's time we got started. Are you ready?"

Thinking of the treacherous rapids ahead, Marianne hoped *Doc* was ready.

Chapter 20
THE RAPIDS
September 26, 1897

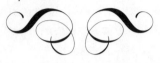

Mosquitoes gave them more trouble than the water did. Marianne slapped at the annoying insects; huge welts blossomed on her hands and face. Relief came only when the wind blew.

After a day of floating and poling on Lake Lindeman, they came upon a gorge about three-quarters of a mile long, with rocks on each side.

The ride through the gorge was smooth until the river split against a large nearly submerged rock. Marianne held her breath as the boat careened and rocked over white swirling rapids. Doc steered and Thomas poled.

"Don't let go of the boat," Doc yelled. Johanna and Marianne gripped the crossbars and looked straight ahead as they rolled and tossed through the rapids.

"This is worse than climbing the mountain," Marianne yelled to Johanna. "At least then my feet were on the ground."

"Hang on!" Johanna shouted.

The boat rocked and rolled. Marianne's clothes were drenched. Her hair was soaked, and the boat was filled with water. Suddenly, they were in smooth water again.

"Well, that wasn't as bad as I had feared," Doc said. "Great practice for Miles Canyon and White Horse Rapids."

"More rapids, worse than those?" Marianne questioned as she and Johanna baled and tried to shake water out of the garments they were wearing. No one had time to answer her.

As they pulled their boat up to shore at Bennett, Marianne saw that, like Lindeman, it was a boat-building settlement.

"Here's where the Chilkoot and White Pass trails converge," Doc explained. "We'll stop just long enough to dry our clothes, eat a meal and rearrange our goods. I'll see what I can find out about conditions ahead."

Thomas followed Doc. Marianne and Johanna built a fire and found a willow thicket where they changed into dry clothes. As they unpacked beef jerky, sourdough biscuits and apple butter, they watched dozens of boats being launched.

"It's twenty-six miles to the end of the lake, and then we're onto a fast moving river," Marianne heard one woman say to another.

Both women, Marianne noticed, struggled with their long mud-spattered skirts, and they looked as though they were still laced into tight corsets.

One of the women had stared at Marianne's trousers. Marianne had heard her say to the other, "Well, I never! Did you see what that young girl was wearing?"

"I'm glad I was wearing trousers," Marianne now said to Johanna. "They're so much more comfortable—even if some folks do stare."

"Yes, I wish I had a pair," Johanna said.

"Each of you take a change of clothing and your sleeping gear and wrap them in these oilskin bags," Doc said when he returned and began checking over the boat. "We're likely to get even wetter."

After their meal, Marianne changed back into her trousers, which by then had dried near the fire. Then she and her companions pushed off again, eager to put behind them the canyon and rapids they'd been hearing so much about.

Their canvas sail saved them labor and gave them confidence as they traveled about twenty feet from shore. The water was calm, so the trip down Lake Bennett was a restful cruise—a relief after the tensions of the trail and the frenzy of boat building.

At one point, a big bull moose crashed out of the willows. Marianne had never seen an animal so majestic yet so homely. Each antler looked like a broad hand with the palm curved and held upward with the margin branching out into prongs. The hairy fold of skin beneath his neck and the hump on his back added to his grotesque appearance.

Thomas reached for his gun, but Doc stopped him. "To wound an animal like that would not only be cruel, but dangerous," he said.

"But I'd kill him for food," Thomas protested.

"How would we handle a thousand pounds of moose meat?" Doc asked. "Besides, it may take more than one shot to fell an animal that big. We won't starve without that moose."

Thomas sighed and put down his gun.

Tossing his huge antlers, the animal disappeared into the thicket. Marianne was glad Thomas hadn't shot the moose.

The next day they continued through calm waters on into the Yukon River until they came to a sharp bend.

"This is the spot Josh told us about," Doc said. "Miles Canyon will be right around the bend." He pulled the boat over to the shore on their right.

"Johanna and Marianne, if you'd be willing to rearrange the gear to keep things as dry as possible, Thomas and I will scout out the river. We'll go along the shoreline to be sure we understand what's ahead. We'll walk the full length of the rapids if necessary. We'll be back in a couple of hours." They headed down the shore.

Marianne hoped Dusty wouldn't show up while Doc and Thomas were gone. She was glad Johanna was with her. Together they marveled at the steep reddish cliffs ahead. Nearby they watched men pacing off distances and pounding wooden stakes with orange flags on them into the ground.

They talked about the dangerous waters ahead. "I heard they call them White Horse Rapids because the foaming water looks like the mane of a horse," Johanna said. "This scenery is so incredible that it's a shame we have to rush through it."

Marianne agreed. "I could enjoy the trip much more if I weren't so worried about Papa."

"But you wouldn't even be making this trip if it weren't for him, would you?"

"I guess you're right, Johanna." Marianne hadn't thought about it that way.

"Have you given any more thought about being a doctor?" Johanna asked.

"Sometimes I imagine what it would be like. I can't believe anyone would object to a woman doctor. After all, aren't women the ones who usually take care of the sick?"

"Indeed, women do *nurse* the sick, but they

aren't allowed to make decisions as a doctor does," Johanna reminded her. "I can understand your wanting to make decisions. That's what I like about having my own restaurant. I can be my own boss, and I feel like I'm meeting a need."

"I'd like to meet the needs of sick folks, Johanna," Marianne said. "Do you think I could persuade Doc to let me help him?"

"Why not ask him?"

To pass the time the two walked up and down the river bank, careful not to get too far from their boat in case Doc and Thomas returned early.

Johanna collected several empty bottles and rinsed them well.

"What will you do with those, Johanna?"

"You never know when an empty bottle might come in handy, Marianne. Why don't you look around for corks?"

In a couple of hours, Doc and Thomas returned.

"I see you've been watching the surveyors," Doc said, nodding toward the crew at work. "They're planning to build a tramway along the canyon. Then no one will have to ride the rapids. That'll make the river journey much safer. Meanwhile, going through the canyon and rapids will be rough, but we can do it. Thomas and I studied the rocks and currents, and talked to several professional boatmen who have been charging folks to be taken through."

"The white water roars through narrow spaces between the rocks," Thomas said to Marianne who was still trying to visualize the mane of a horse.

Johanna looked skeptically at Doc. "Maybe we should walk around the rapids."

"No, we'd have to carry all of our goods some distance through overgrown side trails, and we couldn't do it in one trip. Besides we'd also have to tie ropes to the boat and try to keep it under control as we walked along the riverbank. Just stay calm, and follow my instructions. Let's go!"

Encouraged by Doc's confidence, everyone climbed into the boat and soon they were being swept into the narrow canyon.

As they entered white caps, their scow lurched up and down and from side to side. Marianne stared at two large whirlpools near the cliffs where she saw bits and pieces of broken boats were being ground by the thrashing waters. She clung to her seat. Water splashed into the boat, soaking all of its occupants.

"Pull hard to the right, Thomas!" Doc shouted above the roar as the boat careened from side to side in the seething cauldron. "You're doing fine! Keep going! Johanna and Marianne, don't let go of the boat!"

We may never survive, Marianne thought. If our boat breaks up, I hope the tin can floats and someone sends my letters and journal to Sarah.

"Hang on, we're going to hit this rock broadside!" Doc yelled. Marianne heard the crunch of wood. The tossing and turning continued. She held fast to the cross bar, expecting the boat to overturn. I don't want to die, she thought. I'm too young! She held her breath and gripped the crossbars fiercely. Somehow, the sturdy boat remained upright.

When the waters were quieter, Marianne took a deep breath. Although it had seemed an eternity, the actual ride had taken only a few minutes. Walls of rock, three hundred feet tall with sharp angular projections rose on each side of the river. Marianne and the others were soaked. Their provisions were doused. A foot of water filled the bottom of the boat, yet they were still afloat.

"Grab that bucket and bail!" Doc yelled to Marianne. Johanna was already bailing with a pan. Now Marianne knew why Doc had insisted on unpacking their water pails.

"Thomas, use your pole to keep us from those rocks while I row. We're through the main stretch of rapids, but the danger isn't over yet."

Marianne and Johanna bailed. Doc and Thomas struggled against the surging current.

"Don't stop now!" Doc shouted. "Keep bailing!"

"Thank you, God, for Doc," Marianne whispered to herself as she scooped up pails full of water and threw them overboard. Some folks hadn't been as lucky. Their anguished faces stared at smashed boats and scattered goods littering the shoreline.

"Shouldn't we go back and help?" Marianne asked.

"We can't stop," Doc said.

Once they were out of the canyon, the river swept them on. After much tugging and pulling, they maneuvered into shore, dragged themselves out of the boat and stumbled to the beach.

Doc checked the boat for damage and patted it reverently. "Good Sophia! Together we made it. Now, let's check our gear and get out of these wet clothes."

As they wrestled with their drenched belongings, no one complained. All were happy to be safely through the rapids. Soon they had set up their tents alongside several others who already had campfires blazing. Thomas made a fire, Johanna strung a line between two trees to dry their clothing, and Marianne spread out food.

Marianne's teeth chattered. "Sit down and dry yourself quickly," Johanna instructed. Then she began pouring wet sugar into the bottles she had collected earlier. " We can use this sugar for pancake syrup," she explained.

The bottles had come in handy after all.

Soon Marianne sat shivering in a blanket in front of the fire while her clothes dried. After sipping a cup of soup, she found her waterproof tin and pulled out a wrinkled sheet of paper and a pencil. With her feet warmed by the fire, she wrote:

October 2, 1897
Dear Sarah,

We came through horrendous rapids today. I've never been so frightened. But we survived! Our goods are wet, but we are safe. Some folks weren't so lucky. I'm glad my paper and journal were in a waterproof tin. One of our sacks of sugar got so wet that we are mixing it up as syrup! Did I tell you I'm wearing a pair of Thomas's knickers? Lots of folks don't think this is proper, but it's so much easier to travel in trousers.

Thomas poled the boat like a man. Doc says the rest of the river should be smooth sailing, and we ought to reach Dawson City in about ten days. I hope there's no freeze before then.

Your friend, Marianne.

Chapter 21

DAWSON CITY

October 9, 1897

A s they came round a bend in the river, Thomas cried out, "There's the moose hide shape! We're in Dawson!"

Sure enough, there was the scar on the face of the mountain. The landmark was indeed the color and shape of a moose hide.

Log cabins, wooden shacks and tents, many of which appeared to have been made out of boat sails, lined the shore. Small craft of every kind were beached all along the river bank; some appeared to be makeshift homes.

So this was Dawson City! Marianne was glad to have arrived, but the town was a disappointment. This was nothing like Seattle. She saw no bright lights and colorful streetcars here. Everything was gray and brown, except for the red tunics of several Mounties working around a cluster of log buildings near the river.

The past week on the Yukon had been beautiful but uneventful. Doc's constant concern had been that the river would freeze, but they'd been lucky; the weather had been unseasonably warm, and only a small dusting of snow had fallen.

"Look, there are the North-West Mounted Police

again." Thomas pointed at the men on horseback.
Each policeman wore a red jacket and wide-
brimmed hat. "Remember, we saw them at
Lindeman when we were building our boat?"

"If the Mounties are here, the troublemakers
will lay low," Doc said, "but we'd still better leave
someone to watch our gear when we land."

Doc and Thomas guided their boat to the shore
and climbed out. Johanna and Marianne followed.
Immediately, they found themselves ankle-deep in
mud and slush. Crude hand-lettered signs advertising
HOT COFFEE, SALOON, and BED & BOARD lined the
walkway.

The streets are filled with mud and manure, not
gold, Marianne thought. Horses, dogs and exhausted
stampeders slogged up and down. A tired-looking
woman with straggly hair and tattered blouse was
tacking up a laundry sign. A heavily made-up
woman, wearing a red satin dress and a big black
feather boa, was sitting in the entrance of one of the
tents. Her crossed legs were covered with fishnet
stockings. Marianne saw her wink at Doc as he
walked by. Doc ignored her.

"Thomas, why don't you look for a dry spot to
pitch our tents," Doc directed. "I'll look around and
see what's going on."

"I want to find a site for the restaurant," Johanna
said. "Marianne, would you mind watching our
things?"

"Left behind again," Marianne murmured to
herself. Reluctantly, she went back to the boat,
settled down on the edge of it to watch the people.
At least there's a lot of activity here, she thought.
Several women in fancy dresses walked past, stepping gingerly in fancy shoes. They must make a lot

of money in order to buy such fancy clothes, Marianne thought. She wondered how they had gotten their pretty clothes over the trail and down the river. And why were they here? She guessed they must be dance hall girls.

Several Mounties rode by on horseback. Then Thomas returned announcing he and Johanna had found a suitable place for tents. "Men are everywhere!" he said. "Seems it's too late to stake a claim, but these men are stuck here for the winter. Most have no place to live and not much food."

Soon, Doc, too, was back from his survey of the town. "There are lots of saloons but no grocery stores," he said. "Good thing we brought plenty of food. Folks are going to starve if a steamboat doesn't arrive with food and supplies from St. Michael before freeze-up."

"St. Michael?" Marianne asked.

"A port on the Bering sea," Thomas explained. Then turning to Doc, he asked, "What's keeping the ships? I thought that route from the Pacific Ocean through the Bering Sea and up the Yukon River was the way many folks got here."

"You're right, Thomas," Doc said. "That route is the traditional way, but it's expensive. That's how most of these horses got here. There's not much space available, however; and the Bering Sea and the Yukon River are frozen solid most of the year. The merchants I spoke with don't expect another riverboat until after the ice breaks up next spring. Johanna had the best idea yet—opening a restaurant."

"Johanna's right down the street," Thomas said. "You want to see what she's doing, Marianne? I'll stand watch over our supplies."

Grateful for the opportunity to explore, Marianne followed Doc across the muddy beach and up the street. Johanna bargained with a man, wearing a three-piece suit, who claimed to own the land on which they were standing. This self-appointed realtor, wearing a derby hat, sporting a diamond stick pin in his lapel and smoking a cigar, gestured wildly. Johanna remained calm as she turned and directed a teamster to fetch their provisions from the boat and bring them to the site.

It was incredible how quickly Johanna worked, Marianne thought.

"In exchange for a place to set up my business and our sleeping tents, I've agreed to feed my landlord three meals a day," Johanna said to Doc and Marianne. "We can pitch our tents right here."

"Johanna, you sure know how to handle things," Marianne said. "I wonder if I'll ever be able to barter. If I want to be a doctor, not only will I have to take care of sick people as Doc does, but I'll also have to learn to run a business the way you do."

"You can do it, Marianne," Johanna encouraged. "Think of all the new things you've learned and have accomplished in the past month."

That evening after they'd set up their tents, unpacked their gear and eaten supper, they sat around a campfire. Marianne waited until Doc appeared to be relaxed. Then she said, "Do you like being a doctor?"

"Why do you ask? Do you want to be a doctor, Marianne? Medicine is men's work."

"I've read about women doctors," Marianne said. "Why shouldn't women be allowed to do anything men can do?"

"Actually, this afternoon I learned that a hospital

is being built here in Dawson at the far end of town," Doc said. "I suppose they'll need doctors and nurses. Women can be nurses."

"But what is it really like being a doctor?" Marianne persisted.

Doc hesitated, choosing his words carefully. "Well, after a lot of schooling and exams, you're ready to set up a practice. You feel bad when you can't cure all of your patients. Some die. You get attached to many, and you don't like to ask them to pay when you know they don't have any money."

"But here in the gold fields, there will be lots of money, won't there?" Marianne asked.

Doc shook his head. "Thousands of stampeders are going to be disappointed. What will all those fellows use for money if they didn't bring it with them? Johanna is the one with the gold mine. Folks need to eat, no matter what."

Marianne wondered whether Doc was trying to tell her she should run a restaurant instead of becoming a doctor.

Later, when they were settled for the night in their own tent, Marianne asked Thomas, "When will we start looking for Papa?"

"You stay and help Johanna. I'll start looking tomorrow."

"You get to have all the adventures while I stay here," Marianne protested. "It's not fair!"

"First thing in the morning I'm going to start asking around," Thomas said, ignoring her outburst.

"Well, I can ask too," Marianne said as she crawled into her sleeping roll.

She awoke the next morning in an empty tent, with a snowstorm raging outside. Thomas must have gone to get water.

Chapter 22

THE STORM

Marianne dressed and hurried through the snow to help Johanna feed the hungry men lining up for coffee and oatmeal.

Johanna was bargaining with a native for moose meat. "Yes, I want the whole animal, but it must be *dressed.*" Johanna shook her head. *"You* remove the entrails and hide. Yes, you may keep the hide. I just want the meat."

The native man said, "I will return with meat *dressed* as you say." He turned and merged with the crowd.

"Good morning, Marianne," Joanna said as she tossed a handful of raisins into the kettle. "You're just in time to serve the oatmeal."

I wonder what moose stew tastes like, Marianne thought as she ladled the cereal into customers' bowls and poured hot coffee into their mugs. She listened to the talk.

"All the claims are taken," one of the men grumbled.

"Best thing to do is to hire out to one of the claim owners," another said.

"I'm selling my gear and going home," a man in a denim jacket said.

"Do you have any extra food to sell?" Marianne found herself asking.

"Extra food?" He raised his eyes and looked her squarely in the face. "You don't look hungry to me."

"No, but we could use food for our restaurant."

He hesitated. Then he said, "Well, I guess I could spare some for a young woman as enterprising as you. Looks as though I'd get more money for my food here than in Dyea, and I sure don't want to haul it back over the trail."

"Are you really going home?" she asked.

"Nothing left for me here."

"Have you been where the gold is?" she asked.

"Sure, but I don't have cash to buy out a claim, and I don't want to work for somebody else." He stopped talking and stared at Marianne. "What are you doing here? You're only a child."

"I'm almost thirteen. My brother and I came to find our pa, Robert Carson. Do you know him? Have you seen him?" Marianne waited. He said nothing.

"I'm Marianne Carson," she said finally, to break the silence.

"Jeremy Todd." He held out his hand. Marianne put down her oatmeal ladle. They shook hands. Jeremy stared into space, as if trying to decide what to say. Marianne held her breath.

"My pa is thin and tall like you," she said. "He has dark hair."

Finally Jeremy said, "If he's the man I'm thinking of, your Pa staked one of the first claims on Hunker Creek and was working with his partner upriver, about four miles from here. I heard he had trouble with the partner—the partner was taking more than his share of gold"

"Dusty?" Marianne dared to ask.

Jeremy looked at her. "Yeah, we called him Dusty. Dusty Olsen. Sneaky fellow. The story is that when your Pa confronted him, they had an argument. I heard Dusty took off with their supplies, maybe thinking he could starve your pa and have the claim to himself. Now I hear Dusty's back in town."

"Hmm." Marianne remembered the man poking around their tent at Lake Lindeman. "What does Dusty look like?"

"Thin fellow. Wears corduroy jodhpurs and a leather jacket."

It had to be the same man. "I think my brother is out getting water. I hope he doesn't run into Dusty."

"Did your brother go out alone?"

"I don't know," Marianne said. "I hope Doc went with him." She peeked through the tent opening. Snowflakes continued to fall. Doc stood outside talking to Johanna.

"I don't know what got into him to take off by himself. I just talked to a couple of fellows down at the dock. They saw a kid in a brown coat and tweed knickers headed up the bank of the Klondike before daylight. Not only did he go upriver *alone,* he wasn't dressed for the weather."

Marianne hurried outside, leaving the men to serve the oatmeal themselves. "Maybe it was warm this morning," she said. "How could Thomas know it would turn cold and snow?"

Doc whirled around. "I didn't know you were here, Marianne." He shook his head. "In the Yukon you have to be prepared for anything." He bent down to lace up his boots. "I'm heading out right now to look for Thomas."

"Wait for the Mounties," Johanna begged. "We don't need two people lost in a snowstorm."

Marianne swallowed. She began to see herself left alone. First Papa, and now Thomas. And now Dusty was here in Dawson City. He knew she and Thomas were looking for their pa.

"Get the Mounties to help you," Johanna urged.

"I'll try," Doc said, "but Thomas may be freezing out there. I can't wait."

"I'll go with you, sir," said Jeremy, who had followed Marianne outside. "I'll get my parka and some extra warm clothes for the lad."

"I'd be grateful," Doc said. The men introduced themselves and quickly shook hands. Doc said, "I'll take the small sheet-iron stove, some matches and a couple of blankets." Johanna was already packing food and water. Soon the men were on their way.

"I wish I could go." Marianne watched them leave.

"Stay here and keep yourself warm and well," Johanna said. "We must keep this restaurant going so we can afford to build a cabin."

"But we're going home soon, Johanna, as soon as we find Papa."

"Where *is* home?" Johanna asked.

Marianne pondered the question again. She and Thomas had no relatives in Seattle now. Grandma was gone. Papa probably was somewhere up here in the gold fields.

As she looked at Johanna, Marianne knew she had to accept what she had been hearing. Only people who left Dawson immediately could get Outside before spring. And only those who had enough food would survive the winter.

Chapter 23
WAITING
October 8, 1897

T he day passed slowly, even though Marianne
and Johanna were busy cooking meals and
feeding customers. The thought of spending
the winter in Dawson City, a town of tents and
shacks with hardly any stores and no place to buy
food, was scary.

"At least we have our tents up and enough food
for ourselves and the restaurant," Johanna said to
Marianne as they cleaned up after the noon meal.

But knots twisted in Marianne's stomach. "I
wish Thomas hadn't gone off alone."

"I know how you feel, honey," Johanna said,
putting her arm around her. Marianne laid her head
against Johanna's chest and swallowed hard. Then
she drew away, straightened her shoulders and said,
"Let's get to work."

As the day wore on, Marianne imagined Thomas
buried under the snow. "I don't know what I would
do without him," she said.

"Most things we worry about never happen,"
Johanna said.

"That's what Grandma used to say."

"Your grandma was a wise woman."

After they had finished serving supper, Johanna

said, "Why don't you go to bed early, Marianne? I'll
keep watch for the men."

Marianne headed for her own tent, and then the
tears broke loose. She ran to her bedroll and lay
down, sobbing. Finally she slept.

When she awoke, it was dark. Honky-tonk music
blared from the saloon down the street, making her
head ache; but she knew what she must do. She
bundled up and headed toward the settlement of
buildings they had passed before docking their boat.

She found the cabin marked *NWMP.* A horse
was tied outside.

She was relieved to find a Mountie at his station.
Wearing a uniform with a red jacket and a wide
brimmed hat, he sat at a wooden table.

Marianne peeked in, then gathering courage
and holding her chin high, she strode in, "Excuse me,
Sir."

"Yes?" The voice was businesslike, but pleasant.
"What can I do for you, Miss?" He pulled out his
pocket watch. "It's the middle of the night! Why
aren't you in bed?"

Marianne hesitated, gulped and then began:
"I'm Marianne Carson. I'm camped just down the
street. My pa—his name is Robert Carson—is lost.
My brother has gone to look for him, and now we're
afraid that he's lost, too. Doc Elliott and a man
named Jeremy went to look for Thomas."

She stopped to catch her breath and pushed
her hair back from her face. "They've been gone for
hours. We think Papa's claim is upriver about four
miles. I think his partner Dusty may try to kill him
and take the claim for himself. Can you help?"

The Mountie looked at Marianne. "Slow down.
Now repeat what you just told me." As she spoke, he

scribbled notes. Then he said, "I'll see what I can do."

"When?" Marianne forced herself to say.

"Right away, but first, let me see you back to your camp."

Safely inside her tent, Marianne peeked out and watched the Mountie head back to his cabin. Satisfied he would help, she crawled back into her bedroll. After much tossing and turning, she slept.

Stomping feet awakened her. "We're here, Marianne. We've found Thomas." She recognized Doc's voice. "He's cold, but he's okay."

Half asleep, Marianne grabbed her cape and stumbled out of her tent. Doc and Jeremy were holding up a pale and shivering Thomas.

"He's pretty weak, but we think he managed to escape serious frostbite," Jeremy said. "Another hour or so he might have frozen to death like a fellow I heard about last week.

Marianne hugged her brother. "Oh, Thomas, I'm so glad you're all right, but you're so cold. Come, let's get you warm." She scurried around making tea and warming up the chicken soup she had prepared earlier from dried soup mix. She knew she needed to warm Thomas quickly.

"You shouldn't have gone off by yourself," she scolded. "We were so worried. Why didn't you tell me what you were going to do?"

"Thomas had traveled about two miles up the road," Jeremy said. "We found him huddled under some bushes where he'd been trying to make a shelter out of branches and snow. This is our first big storm of the winter, so there was hardly enough snow to build a shelter."

Johanna brought blankets and wrapped them around Thomas.

Doc turned to Thomas. "You're darn lucky, boy. I know you want to find your Pa, but be patient and we'll help you."

"I guess leaving town without survival gear was a pretty stupid thing to do," Thomas admitted. He took a sip of tea and tasted the soup.

After some color had returned to Thomas's face, Marianne asked, "Did you find any signs of Papa?"

"The Mounties have organized a search party," Doc said. "I wonder who alerted them. We met them heading on up the trail. They told us they're looking for Dusty, too. They think he's hiding out some-where not far from your Pa's claim."

Marianne didn't tell them she had gone to see the Mounties herself.

Johanna prepared hot lemonade and offered it to Doc and Marianne as well as to Thomas. "I'm turning in now," she said. "Call me if you need me." Marianne and Doc sat with Thomas until he dozed off.

When Thomas appeared to be comfortable and breathing normally, Marianne said to Doc, "This is taking time from your work. If you weren't out chasing after Thomas and trying to find Papa, you could be looking for gold."

"Actually I'm thinking I'll be practicing medi-cine instead of looking for gold."

"But we're keeping you from setting up your medical practice as well."

"I'll get to that soon enough. They need doctors so badly in the hospital here I think they'll waive the fact I'm not licensed in the Yukon. I'll be paid a

salary, and won't be bothered by billing and paper-
work."

"Maybe I could help you," Marianne suggested.

"Help me? If you can escape the food tent,
perhaps."

"Oh, I can do that. Johanna won't need me
forever." Well *maybe* Johanna wouldn't need her.

"What exactly do you think you could do at the
hospital?" Doc asked.

"You could teach me to roll bandages, sterilize
instruments, take the patient's pulse and tempera-
ture. I could learn as we go."

"We'll see," Doc said. "For now though, take care
of your brother. Keep him quiet and give him lots of
liquids."

Marianne nodded. She could take care of
Thomas. And she'd show Doc that she could care
for others as well. But she wished Doc and Jeremy
would hurry and help the Mounties find Papa.

As if reading her mind, Doc said, "We'll join the
Mounties and go look for your Pa right away. You
tend to Thomas. This will be a good opportunity to
practice your doctoring skills."

After they left, Marianne shivered, wrapped
herself in her bedroll, sat down beside Thomas and
imagined herself in medical school.

Chapter 24
PAPA
October 9, 1897

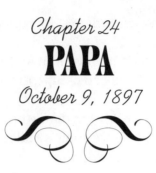

Waking to the aroma of garlic and basil, Marianne jumped up, dressed and ran to the tent next door.

"What's for breakfast?" she asked.

"You missed it! "Johanna smiled. "You had quite a sleep, but we have a surprise for you!"

A thin, tired-looking, bearded man stepped out from behind the makeshift restaurant table. Marianne stared at him. She must be dreaming. Her Pa didn't have a beard, but this man did. Then she saw his eyes. There was no doubt who he was.

"Papa!" Marianne cried, flinging her arms around her father. "It's really you. I'm so glad we found you."

"Seems as though *I found you*," Papa said. "Let me look at you. Why, you've grown three inches at least. You're a young lady now in spite of the britches."

Marianne blushed. She had forgotten about the trousers. "Yes, Papa. I am nearly grown." Tears of relief rolled down her cheeks, and she buried her head in her father's chest.

"And trousers? I'll have to get used to those. They're certainly practical here, aren't they?" He took Marianne's hands in his, stepped back and looked at her from head to foot, shaking his head.

"Now where's Thomas? I heard he came looking for me. Foolish thing to do, but I'd have done the same for him. Where is that rascal?"

"This way, Papa." Marianne led him back to their own tent. "Yes," she agreed, "Thomas was foolish, but he was only trying to help."

She watched as Papa woke Thomas and hugged him. Then she stood by, happy to have both her brother and her papa safe and near her.

"Oh, Papa, are you all right?" Marianne asked. "We haven't heard from you in a whole year."

"I'm fine," Papa said, "and I sure did miss you kids. I've written you, but the mail just isn't reliable here. And none goes out from Dawson during the winter. Probably by now my letters to you are in Seattle.

"But hold on just a minute, Gal. How'd you kids get here? Where's your grandmother? I can't believe she let you leave Seattle."

"Grandma died," Marianne said. Then she and Thomas told Papa about Grandma, their trip on the steamship to Dyea, the hike over the Chilkoot Trail, and the boat ride to Dawson.

Papa shook his head in disbelief. "First you lost your mother. Then your mother's mother. I'm so sorry."

"Tell us what happened to you, Papa," Marianne urged.

"I'll tell you while we eat. I sure could use something besides sourdough and beans! Is that stew I smell?"

"It's moose stew, Papa," Marianne said. "How about some fresh bread and blueberry jam to go with the stew? Do you like moose?"

"Sounds good to me. But where'd you get it? I haven't seen any animals around here lately. I think the early prospectors got them all."

"Johanna paid a big price for the meat. She got it from a Native who brought it downriver. Now you'll have to follow me to the food tent if you want some stew."

Marianne led the way. Her Pa and Thomas followed. Johanna, Doc and Jeremy were already at the table. They, too, wanted to hear Pa's story.

Pa savored the food, laid down his fork and began his tale. "Dusty and I met in Dyea. We pooled our resources, but when we arrived at Fortymile, he took off with a miner who already had a rich claim. Then there was this big strike here in the Klondike, so I rushed over and staked one of the first claims."

"Gee! "Thomas exclaimed. "That must have been exciting!"

"Yes, but I didn't know if I'd strike a vein, and it wasn't easy working by myself. After a few days, though, as soon as I found good pay dirt, back comes Dusty, ready to be my partner again. I hesitated since he'd let me down once, but I needed the help. So I decided to give him another chance.

"We worked hard, but there just wasn't enough gold fast enough to suit Dusty. By the time we had a good cleanup, he wanted to buy me out. I refused. He got angry. One morning I woke to find he had left the cabin and taken all of his grub and most of mine. If it hadn't been for the sourdough starter I'd hidden and that one last sack of flour and bag of beans, he'd have wiped me out."

"Sourdough really did save your life," Marianne said. "Doc told us how important it is."

"It certainly is important," Pa agreed. "I soon realized Dusty had also taken off with the gold pokes."

"Pokes?" Marianne questioned.

"Those little bags we use to carry gold nuggets. He took them all. I was left with barely enough food and firewood and all this pay dirt to work the gold out of over the winter. It was obvious he thought I'd either freeze to death or starve. Then he'd come back and take over the claim."

"How rotten!" Marianne said.

"He's a rat," Thomas said.

"Have you seen him lately?" Doc asked.

"He's in jail, thanks to the Mounties," Papa said. "They found him last night prowling around my place, and arrested him. Marianne, you were right to go to the Mounties."

Thomas, Doc, Johanna and Jeremy all stared at Marianne.

"You went to the Mounties?" Johanna said.

Marianne nodded, uncomfortable to be the center of attention.

"You, my shy little sister?" Thomas said.

"Yes."

"What did you tell the Mounties?" Doc wanted to know.

"That someone might be trying to kill Papa."

"If you hadn't alerted them, I don't know what would have happened," Papa said. "First, they captured Dusty. Then they brought me into town by dog sled."

"What are you going to do now, Pa?" Thomas asked.

Marianne held her breath, waiting for his answer.

"Stick around here and tend to my claim, I guess. I need to take food and firewood back to the cabin. I've found good color, but I'll have to keep bringing pay dirt up out of the shaft so I can sluice out the gold in the spring."

"You mean *we*," Thomas said. "I'll help you, Pa."

"I could help, too, Papa," Marianne chimed in.

"You two had better stay here in Dawson and go to school."

"Papa, I don't think there is a school here." Marianne said. "Why don't you stay in town and be our teacher. You could *start* a school." Marianne hugged him. "Oh, Papa. Please."

"Wait a minute," Jeremy interrupted. "Are you a teacher? I thought you looked familiar. Weren't we in the same geography class at teacher's college?"

"Now that you mention it, I believe you're right," Pa said. "I thought you looked familiar. Where have you been all this time?"

"I soon decided I wasn't cut out to teach geography but thought I'd go see the world for myself," Jeremy said. "I'd had some mining experience, so I started with Canada and here I am." He repeated what he'd told Marianne earlier about not having enough cash to buy a claim and not wanting to work for someone else for wages.

"I'm not sure I'm cut out for mining," Pa said. "Jeremy, you're the one with the mining experience. You should be the one to spend the winter on the claim. If I make you a partner and I stay in town to teach, I could build a cabin for all of us. In summer Thomas and I could work the claim with you."

Marianne said, "And I can help Johanna with her restaurant."

"That would be great," Johanna said.

"And maybe between meal times Doc will let me help him with his patients." She glanced at Doc.

He nodded. "I think I can find a place for you."

"Thank you, thank you!" Marianne jumped up and hugged Doc.

"You will be the teacher here, won't you, Pa?" Marianne held her breath.

"My, my," Papa said. "Teaching school surely would beat spending the winter on the claim. The pay might not be as good, but the company will be better. What do you think, Jeremy?"

"Sounds like a good plan to me."

Marianne danced up and down and hugged Papa, Thomas, Johanna, Doc and even Jeremy.

Tonight, she would write another letter to Sarah.